BABY LOST

FROM THE DIARY OF
A NEONATAL NURSE

A NOVEL
BY LEILANI RULAND

For Frederick, my husband and best friend

And with love to Heather, Shane, Brett, and Brittney

July 3, 8:00 p.m. The Nursery

Annie ran wildly, the new intern right behind her, as they headed toward the sound of a heart dropping its beat. Jessie's face had already changed color when they reached his cubicle. The intern placed his stethoscope against the tiny chest as Annie turned the oxygen up to one-hundred percent. "He's blue," she said.

"Jesus," the intern's face was pale, "I can't hear his breath sounds. I can't tell if the tube is in the right place." His hands shook. "I'm not used to touching such a tiny baby."

"Calm down," Annie said. "Think! You're a doctor. Use your head. You know what to do." She grabbed the wall phone and dialed the operator. "Page Doctor Phillips. Stat. NICU." She quickly donned rubber gloves and began to suction the baby's lungs as another minute crawled by.

Jessie's heart rate was down to fifty.

Another nurse ran into the cubicle. "I'm here," Tess said, "I'll record and draw up drugs."

"Where the hell is Phillips?" the intern asked. "My resident is in surgery."

They saw the frothy mucus with streaks of red come up the endotracheal tube. "Call the lab and order blood," he said to Annie. "How much does he weigh?"

"Two kilos," Annie answered. "You'd better push some fluid."

Tess handed them the drug filled syringes.

The tiny baby was losing his battle.

Annie disconnected the ventilator and started bag-breathing, and still the heart rate continued to drop. Tess took over the bagging as Annie began compressions, one finger pushing gently on the fragile chest.

Jessie's father rushed into the room, panting loudly as he pushed his wife out of his way. "We were eating. We heard the page. What happened?" There was a new IV line in Jessie's scalp that Annie had placed earlier in the shift.

"What the hell happened to his hair?" He stood behind Annie still breathing heavily. She could smell his hot alcoholic breath on her neck.

"I'll page Phillips again," Tess said.

Annie turned the baby slightly and bright blood gushed out of his mouth. His heart rate dropped to forty as he turned bluer. The tiny mouth twitched and he began sucking on the tube in his throat.

"Jesus," said the intern, "he's having a seizure." He started to say something else, but Annie shushed him. "Give the drugs. Stop talking." She kept her face in tight control as she motioned for Tess to push the panic button.

Immediately, the operator called out, "Code Blue. Code Blue. NICU."

The mother whimpered, pleaded, "Jessie. Jessie. Where's Doctor Phillips? Why doesn't he come?"

Jessie's father spat out curse words and tried to put his arm around his wife's shoulder, but Mary pushed him out of the way. She gripped the sides of the warming bed with both hands. "No, Jessie, no—"

Annie silently prayed. *Please, please, please, Phillips. Where in the hell are you?*

She turned and saw his shadow as Doctor Phillips entered the room. He barely glanced at the baby and turned to the intern. "How many rounds of drugs have you given, son?"

"Three rounds, Sir," the young man whispered, the panic still in his voice.

The heart rate was down to ten, and the alarms continued shrieking.

Phillips ran his hand gently over Jessie's stomach; it was now distended and tight as a drum. The baby was still—his eyes wide open.

Phillips deliberately ignored Jessie's father as he patted Mary's shoulder. "I'm sorry, mama." He reached over and turned off the alarms.

He touched the arm of the helpless intern who was still pushing a small syringe filled with an emergency drug. "Stop now," he said. His voice was high-pitched and strange. "I just saw his lab work. His gut is dead. He didn't have a prayer."

He gently brushed the top of Jessie's head.

"Pronounce him, son. It will be your first death."

And then Phillips was gone.

Jessie's mother bent over her baby and smoothed down the one pitiful clump of hair that lay over his ear. She traced the baby's mouth, and closed the sightless eyes. She stepped back and raised her hand to her own face. A streak of Jessie's blood appeared on her cheek.

Jessie's father turned to Annie and she saw the hate in the black dilated eyes.

Then . . . there was only the sound of a mother's broken heart.

July 4, 3:30 a.m. Carpenter Street

A police car's siren brought Jessie's father out of his drunken stupor. He sat up, knocked the empty beer can off the bed, heard it roll across the floor and smack into the wall.

The police car's red and blue lights flashed briefly through the torn curtain hanging over the open window, and then disappeared.

He heard a rustling noise, a snickering. A child's voice yelled, "You in there old drunk?" Giggles and then a loud bang as a firecracker exploded. Those damn neighborhood kids had been pestering him since midnight. His head ached from the liquor and all the fireworks.

He turned on the light. A family of cockroaches scurried away and marched single file down the side of the night stand.

A stab of pain made him grab his head.

He remembered.

His baby—Jessie—was dead.

Mary was gone.

She had left him again.

The rage that quieted only when his abused body slept pulled him fully awake. The heat was stifling in the untidy rented room. He was covered in sweat, the sheet wrapped around him like a wet towel. He had not bathed in a week.

He was a house painter, odd job repairman, master of no trade but alcohol.

His money was gone and so was his beer. He rubbed his swollen eyes and lay back upon his pillow.

The loss filled his soul, his head pounded, he no longer reasoned like a sane man. A groan escaped from his lips.

He needed a plan.

A face surfaced in his mind. The one the nurses jokingly called the blue-eyed albino.

Doctor Phillips, the white-haired, pale skinned doctor with the blue eyes. As the face materialized he remembered how the doctor's lips always curled into a wide disgusted look every time he met him.

His body shook with renewed anger.

I'll kill him! The scream was silent.

He lit a cigarette with sweaty fingers that slipped on the lighter. Many thoughts kaleidoscoped through his crippled mind.

"I'll kill him!" He said it out loud for the first time. The words echoed off the wall.

He inhaled deeply and watched the cigarette's glow as another firecracker went off under his window. A small rock flew into the room through the open window. He didn't react, but heard the pounding of feet running away.

He felt the cigarette burning into his flesh.

He didn't flinch until the pain was unbearable.

He knew what he had to do.

5:45 a.m. The Parking Garage

Annie Barker drove onto the ramp of the Children's Hospital parking garage, and lowered the window of her new white Ford. The heat poured into the car. For a week now the daily temperature had gone over the one-hundred degree mark. The Midwestern city baked like the world's largest pie.

Everyone suffered.

Annie shoved her keycard into the slot and the gate malfunctioned. A familiar voice squawked from the intercom, "Just a minute."

A horn blew behind her. She leaned out her window and spotted Guy, a respiratory therapist, her favorite. She remembered their first meeting. He had assisted her in a Code Blue, and when the baby was stable she had turned to him and said, "Hi, I'm Annie." "My name's Guy," he said, as he shook her hand. "I'm young. I'm Black. I'm gay." She burst out laughing and they had been friends ever since.

From her window she could see the big silver cross dangling from his right ear. No jewelry was allowed on duty, but she suspected that since today was a holiday, many rules would be broken. He drove a battered Volkswagen Beetle painted bright green. On the bumper was a sticker: SOMEONE I

LOVE WAS MURDERED. His former partner died of AIDS.

The gate was going halfway up and then back down. Annie wiped the perspiration from her upper lip, grateful that Guy was working again today.

They had parted only hours before after working through an evening of hell. A respirator had stopped working on one of her critical patients, and Guy had finally managed to help her switch the baby to a different machine. Equipment breakdown was a major headache. Machines had to be monitored as closely as patients. She wanted to tell that fact to the general public, to the people who thought that nurses made too much money. Everyone was always asking her: "What do you do all day, feed babies?" Her eighty-seven year old neighbor had never spent a day in a hospital, but she had told Annie, "I love nurses. I hope that if I ever have to go to the hospital, a nurse will take time to sit with me, and put a cold cloth on my head."

Annie had answered her, and not too kindly, "I hope that they will know how to work my respirator."

Guy yelled, "I thought you were going to call in sick?"

She laughed at that remark as the gate went up. Last week Guy had told her he and his new partner were buying a house, and she had told him that she was going to retire. Her twenty-year anniversary was coming up. Guy was the only one who new this.

Her signed resignation was in her purse. Once it was posted on the memo board everyone would know. Proper procedure, that's how they did things on her unit.

One small thought hindered her final decision. Two days ago, she had been offered a position on the hospital's new ethics board. This board would supposedly help parents and staff make wiser medical decisions. A baby's long drawn out death affected them all. Some of the doctors and nurses disagreed with the board's new purpose saying they were trying to "play God."

Jackson wanted her to stop working all together. They had no children. "Let's do some traveling," he said, "while we're still young. We can walk. We have good eyes. It will be fun." They had laughed together. He was actually five years younger than she, trim and muscular, a long distance trucker. Just when she thought she would never marry, he had come along and changed her mind.

Two days ago, she had been standing at her kitchen window musing about the increasingly huge familiar groundhog crossing their scorched grass. "I've gained five pounds this summer," she lamented to Jackson, unhappy about the extra weight on her slim figure.

"Take an early retirement," Jackson said. "We can go to China." His great-grandfather had emigrated from there, and Jackson wanted to find the small village where he had been born. They were taking a home language course now, and even had a tape-player in the bathroom.

Annie shook off her thoughts as she drove around the second level of the garage searching for a parking space. She found one next to a shiny blue Mercedes with FANCY on the license plate. *So, Fancy was already here and probably eating a big breakfast in the cafeteria.*

As she parked her car, an old battered Chevy pulled in three spaces down. Her heart leaped in her throat as she heard the noise of the car's familiar engine die down. He was driving the twenty-year-old car.

It seemed like only yesterday that he had gone from her life—Mark Blair. All week she had been preparing herself for their first meeting. She practiced, repeatedly, in front of a mirror, exactly what she would say.

She felt her face flame as she got out of her car and locked the door. She wanted to hurry away, but she couldn't. She walked to his car and waited. She watched the tall gangly surgeon climb out of the car, his long legs encased in khaki pants. The brick-red curly hair, his trademark, was a little gray around the edges now. He was much leaner than she remembered, but still elegant. He wore a white shirt, open at the neck. His blue eyes darkened considerably in the early morning light that filtered through the open slots of the garage wall.

She was the first to speak and heard the tremble in her voice. "When are you going to get a new car?" She held out her hand. "Welcome back."

He gripped her hand and an electric shock went through her as the long, sensitive, surgeon's fingers curled around her palm. His face was full of surprise, pleasure, and maybe a little fear. She noted the fine crinkly lines around his eyes, the cheeks free of wrinkles, and the deep familiar cleft in his chin that widened as he smiled.

He let go of her hand and patted the top of the car, the old station wagon with its blue paint faded and peppered with rust. "I've got a new car, but this one was always my baby. I can still change my own oil. The new cars are too complicated. They need mechanics." He chatted away without looking at her.

"Bet those mechanics can't sew up a hole in a tiny gut," she said. They looked at each other, but neither spoke for several seconds.

As the early morning sunlight bathed his features in a gentle way, the past washed over them like it was only yesterday.

"How are you Annie?" His gaze was steady now, "How many years have we lost?"

"More than twenty," she said in a soft voice.

He sighed. "That long? And have the years been good to you Annie?" His deep musical voice was the same and she was glad.

"Very good," she said. "I heard you were coming back, but I didn't think I'd see you on a holiday." And not this holiday she thought, a holiday they had shared on their last day together.

Pain flashed across his features, and she knew he too remembered that July Fourth. He paled and looked away for a moment.

"I was proud when I heard you were going to head the new trauma team. It's going to have a much needed role in this special hospital." He colored at her words but she didn't care, she was sincere. She was back in control of her emotions.

"The first day of new interns always scares the hell out of me," he sighed. "I wasn't sure I would come back but I had some good memories here, some wonderful times. And it's a top hospital now, so my research will be appreciated. I'll try to hold on to that and somehow let go of the past." His voice trailed off and then he brightened. "I heard you were a writer, already a book of poetry published. Wow!"

"Thank you." She was suddenly shy. "And you with five books under your belt."

"Six," he said, "but who's counting? Ah, Annie, that last time we stood in this area it was a gravel lot. I asked you to come away with me, remember? You said you couldn't come."

"I would have been excess baggage, you already had a wife."

Still, they had those five golden days that late July. She had been young and single, and he had strutted around like a proud angry ostrich when his wife had left him. Annie couldn't wait for him to finish those last few weeks, and then his wife—dead—under mysterious circumstances. It was then that thoughts of their future scared the hell out of her. He was gone, suddenly, even before his residency ended, without a goodbye. And to her, this said, it was over.

She had returned all his letters, unopened. Her roommate had been instructed to say she was out when he called. The letters and the calls finally stopped and she had gone on with her life.

They were saved from further speech by the loud thumping of a helicopter as Life Flight landed on the roof.

His head jerked up as he said, "Trauma!" He touched her arm. "Please, let's talk later." He turned and raced toward the stairs with incredible speed. At the door he paused, lifted an arm high in farewell, and disappeared from her view.

Annie shook off all thoughts about him as she hurried through the underground tunnel to the hospital. Most of the staff had never known him. She would protect him from the past.

She climbed the stairs to the main lobby. She had been called from sleep by a frantic night nurse. "Can you come in early? I've had four ill calls. We are short-staffed."

Again, and this was the Fourth of July.

The weatherman had predicted storms all week, and a big one that would hit sometime today when the heat wave lifted. There had already been tornadoes in the South. Every time they predicted a big storm the staff would jokingly call it 'The Big One,' just like the quake that was always threatening California.

This was not the biggest problem Annie was concerned with. The new interns would have their first day today. The one who had shadowed her last evening was not even supposed to be on duty. He had been so eager to start work that his resident welcomed his help and then had left him in charge. When Jessie crashed, the intern had been scared to death.

Still, she knew he had made no mistakes. Jessie was doomed, just like Phillips said, but why let that poor young doctor suffer through that death on his own. She would never understand why hospitals put new doctors to work on a holiday. She had often told Doctor Phillips that it was a stupid way to train doctors. He always assured her that it was the best way, usually rationalizing that was the way it had always been done, and adding that new interns start on the first of July, and that working this holiday was part of their job.

"But it's still not safe," Annie always replied.

She reached the elevators and found a group of new interns, huddled together, looking confused.

"Excuse me, ma'am," one of them called out to her, a short thin man with bad skin and long black hair. He looked all of sixteen. She hated that ma'am word, but she stopped to listen to his plea.

"Where's the cafeteria? We're new here." He blushed as the group laughed.

"I would never have guessed," Annie said, laughing with them. "Don't they give you a hospital tour?"

She looked over the group. There were three women—two well-dressed still in their street clothes. The oldest, with gray bangs, her face permanently lined with fatigue, smiled at Annie. Four others, men, all needing shaves, were dressed in the rumpled green scrubs that belonged to surgery. Annie wondered if they had been up all night just worrying about today.

"How many docs did we get this year?" Annie asked.

"Thirty-one," someone answered.

Annie was shocked. She had seen a memo stating that the hospital was cutting back on the medical staff this year and the new interns would be going back to thirty-six-hour duty, but thirty-one would not be adequate, not for a hospital this large.

She pointed out the artwork along the wall. "Follow the art and you'll find the food."

• • •

Annie was the only one in the nurses lounge, and she quickly changed into her scrubs, and put on her tennis shoes. She longed for a cigarette but there was no longer any smoking in the hospital. As she started to close her locker, she saw the long white envelope in her purse. She hesitated. Should she push it under the head nurse's door now, or wait until later?

Later! She slammed the locker door.

6:50 a.m. The Nursery

Annie pushed the automatic door opener, entered the nursery, and was cheered upon her arrival. Two of the night nurses yelled in unison, "She's here! Soon, we'll be out of here!"

Annie felt elated. She was back again walking on sacred ground in the recently renovated intensive care unit for newborns. She never failed to get this feeling. The love of her profession propelled her forward.

The nursery was bright and cheerful, done in soft light colors. She saw the animal patterns that criss-crossed the walls giving the unit the homey appearance that a baby nursery should have. She had been asked to help in choosing the border. Her first choice had been panda bears, but the administration vetoed that.

The nursery was divided into sections that were officially called pods. There were three separate isolation rooms, the walls glassed for visibility. It was much larger than the old nursery, and the staff affectionately dubbed it the Food Club Warehouse.

The nurses station was in the front on the left, always brightly lit, and set off by a waist-high counter. There was a bank of telephones, a large computer system, and wall-to-wall shelves filled with numerous

15

hospital forms. The chairs were heavily padded for comfort.

One wall enclosed the hospital's pneumatic tube system. The desk was L-shaped, and on one side hung a large bulletin board. On this board in various colors of erasable ink were the names of the patients, their caregiver, and the names of the interns and residents. Annie quickly checked the names. More than half of the babies had a red star denoting that they were critically ill.

Jessie's cubicle was still empty.

The night charge nurse was behind the desk. "Give me a couple of minutes, Annie, I'm not quite ready to give you report." Annie saw that she was sorting and filling a pile of syringes, the dreaded chore that had to be done several times during a shift. The pungent smell of Lysol was in the air and Annie's shoes squeaked as she walked. She dodged the 'wet floor' sign, almost stumbling. "Why do they mop these floors when we're so busy?" She looked up and caught the grin from the housekeeper, a young girl with her face heavily rouged. "Sorry," Annie mumbled an apology. She turned and called back to Stephanie, the night nurse, "I'll just go for a minute to Del-baby."

"Today's her six-week birthday," Stephanie responded, "and I assigned her to you."

Annie loved the little girl. All the nurses loved her. Even the doctors continued to be amazed at the tiny black girl. She was their miracle baby.

The baby lay curled on her side, with a soft blanket-roll folded around her forming a nest. She was naked, lying on a piece of lamb's wool, only a paper diaper under her. Her little butt was arched in the air. The positive butt sign, the doctors called it. Annie washed her hands and put on a pair of rubber gloves. She opened the door of the isolette and removed the paper diaper. She weighed it on a tiny scale, marked down the amount, and replaced it with a dry one.

She rubbed the ringlet-covered head, and no longer felt the melancholy ache in her heart.

"Deltiffinase," she crooned softly, thinking of the poem she was working on at home. "I call your name and the sound rolls off my tongue like a foreign language."

She sang to the baby, felt the sweet breath against her arm. It was like the kiss of a tiny butterfly.

"Hallelujah," Annie said. "You are breathing on your own and off that nasty respirator for three days now."

Annie read her chart: two pounds, two ounces.

Deltiffinase curled her body slowly back into a round ball, letting the warm misted oxygen blow into her face. Her tiny chest moved in rhythm with the heartbeat that marched across the monitor over her bed.

"Don't breathe too fast, girl," she chided the baby.

She patted the downy skin. "You're in my care today. So be a good girl. No medical emergencies, please." She felt a sudden ache as she marked on the chart. *Is this what I really want to give up? Leave this baby? All these babies? I'm not old. I'm not too old.* And yet she was the oldest neonatal nurse here. Most of the staff were a lot younger, in their twenties and thirties. There was always a new face. This kind of nursing took its toll, Annie knew.

Dying babies, sometimes every day, sometimes nurses moved on without looking back. Still, these were the ones that needed you, someone to hold them, tell them goodbye. She was glad she had chosen to be here.

She charted on the nursing notes that the baby's color was pink, at least it was pink under the pearl-sized nail beds of her chocolate skin. She was a shade darker than her mother.

Annie remembered the night that the baby was born.

"We're bringing one in to die," the squad's driver lamented over the telephone as he gave out the birth history.

Born at home to a fifteen-year-old who had not revealed her pregnancy to her family. No prenatal care. The baby had arrived in the nursery, a one pound quivering mass of skin and bones. She was so cold that her body temperature had not registered on the thermometer. Twenty-four weeks gestation, her eyelids still fused like those of a kitten.

All the statistics were against her survival.

They placed her on a radiant warmer, added extra heat lamps, let her breathe in a high level of oxygen, and tried not to handle her.

"She'll die," the staff doctor in charge said. "Her lungs are too immature to put her on a respirator." The baby continued to gasp for breath as she struggled to live.

She would not die.

The doctors and nurses argued about her treatment. While usually agreeing among themselves, they knew there was always a fine line between doing too much and not doing enough, especially on these tiny fetuses.

Too much or too little?

What to do?

Her second night, the resident on duty was a cross-cover doctor from the ICU. He made the decision to go ahead and put her on the respirator. "I can't watch her struggle any longer," he said. "I took an oath to do no harm." Later, he would confess to Annie that it was the smallest breathing baby he had ever seen. Annie remembered threading a needle into the fragile leg vein. It had taken more than one try and each needle stick left a big bruise.

After she was intubated, the baby did not fight the respirator, and her blood gases amazed them as the tiny girl stabilized. The doctor ordered an intravenous solution and antibiotics.

"The rest is up to the baby," he said, "and God."

Annie remembered how incredible she felt the next time she walked into the nursery and found the baby still alive. She was not only alive, but they were weaning her oxygen.

Still such a pathetic sight—she lay covered in bruises in various shades of purple and blue.

Every day was harrowing. Her lungs were troublesome. The oxygen requirements went up and down like a roller coaster.

Annie wanted this baby to live.

Her mother breezed in one morning, a gum-chewing teenager, who made jokes about her real Barbie Doll as she gave the baby a name that was longer than her tiny body.

Deltiffinase.

The name meant nothing. "Made it up," she said. "I liked the sound of it. And so does my boyfriend."

The nurses began to joke among themselves. In secret, they called her Del-baby.

Joke or not, the tiny bit of humanity made it through the two weeks. Her skin turned bright orange, and she was placed under two fluorescent lights with her eyes covered to bring down the dangerous bilirubin level in her blood.

On her eighth day of life, she almost gave up her fight. Her heart stopped four times. The doctor in charge that day was experienced. He did an emergency cut-down on a tiny vein. Before he started, Annie fought viciously for pain medication.

"Even if it kills her," Annie said. "We can't let her suffer any more than she already has."

All the nurses ganged up on the doctors and demanded that new guidelines be drawn up for the use of pain medications on their tiny infants. The problem was still stuck 'in committee,' but Del-baby got her pain medication.

That same night, over a seven hour block of time, Deltiffinase blew four separate holes in her lungs. Each time the weary blue-shirted intern sutured the chest tube in place, he swore it would be the last, saying, "I can't find another spot to make a hole." Annie worked a double shift that night and every free minute she was at the baby's bedside, guarding her like a sentry guards a queen.

Later that night, the mother and grandmother had come into the nursery. They were both chewing gum. The snapping sound grated on Annie's nerves. The grandmother, a hard-faced, rather young woman, perhaps in her late thirties, was dressed in black skin-tight pants and high heels. Her hair was piled high on her head, and her huge gold earrings flashed and danced in the artificial light.

The round-faced mother wore a childish animal print shirt, cut-off shorts, bobby sox, and expensive black tennis shoes. Her fine silver bracelets jangled and clinked as she put her hand to her mouth to pop her gum in and out.

She never touched her baby.

"Who does she look like, mommy?"

The grandmother shook her head, "She don't look like no baby I ever seen before."

Annie had watched their eyes dart around the pod, taking in the forms of the other infants.

"She looks like the smallest one here."

"Not quite," Annie had lied. She wondered why they irritated her so much. She was certainly used to teenage mothers.

The two of them fingered the little pink dress that was hanging on the IV pole. Annie knew that a night nurse had bought it.

The grandmother twisted the knob on the baby's music box, held it to her ear for a few seconds, and then put it back in the isolette.

When the mother left the room, saying she was going for something to drink, the grandmother had turned to Annie.

"I don't want her to hear this," the woman said. She kept her head down. "We won't be back. The baby's not going to make it, and I don't want my child to go through any more."

"I think you need to talk to your social worker," Annie had answered as the woman walked away from the bedside without a backward glance, dismissing the baby as if she was damaged goods that they couldn't keep.

The social worker had then filed for a court order to protect the child, but it had not been necessary, for the family simply disappeared—moved without leaving a forwarding address. "If the baby lives, we'll find the mother," someone from social services had told the distressed nurses.

An alarm sounded, and Annie pulled her thoughts back to the present. She pressed a foam-covered lead back in place over the tiny heart and whispered to the baby, "On your tenth day of life, you opened your eyes."

The baby's eyes were open now, and Annie touched the baby's hand and said, "Happy birthday, Deltiffinase."

The miniature fingers closed around Annie's thumb.

"You are incredible, and you are still here."

Annie hurried down the hallway to the nursing station.

Stephanie came and plopped down beside her. She was an efficient nurse, and had worked on the night shift for several years. Annie thought the night nurses were special, because she had been a night nurse until she had married.

Stephanie was a striking brunette, always immaculate, never hurried. She had a plain everyday face, until she smiled. Her eyes would soften with that special glow like the one in a child's eyes when it learns it can walk. She had three small children and a disabled husband on a military pension, but she never complained.

"We have twenty-one babies," she said.

"So, not only in charge, but a patient assignment," Annie smiled. "How many nurses did you call before you asked me to be in charge?"

Stephanie flushed, caught off guard, "Only you." She was always truthful. "And if you get another admission, you'll have to figure out who can admit it. You're all going to be on overload. Every time that damn phone rang, I prayed that it wouldn't be about another mother in premature labor."

Stephanie's stomach rumbled. "Do you have anything to eat? My lunch is wasted in the lounge. I had to beat on Kerry's lungs so many times last night that my food went cold."

Annie fished a cinnamon drop out of her pocket. She always carried candy since she had given up cigarettes. Everyone knew this. Although the staff wasn't allowed to eat in the unit because of newly enforced safety regulations, everyone did it on occasion. There was an immediate fine, on the spot, if an administrator caught someone with food, but it was highly unlikely that an administrator would work on this holiday.

Stephanie pounced on the candy and said, "Thank you for coming in early. If I had to stay over one more night this week, Joe said he was going to divorce me. The baby has been fussy with an ear infection and he doesn't sleep." She stuffed the candy into her mouth like a wicked child and wiped her hand on her scrub pants. Her hair was pulled back into a ponytail and her lipstick was fresh. Not one of her red-polished nails was chipped, and yet Annie knew she was not a shirker. She was a member of the group they called 'The Hardcore.' They were always dependable and dedicated, and most of them worked on the night shift. Annie felt lucky to be included in their group.

Stephanie went over the Kardex quickly, skimming over the stable babies first, their lab work, and the changes in their conditions. She sighed when she got to the last name.

"Kerry Dawson is trying to die."

"Every nurse's nightmare," Annie said, underlining the baby's name on her charge sheet. She was the most chronically ill baby of all their patients now since Jessie was dead.

Born too soon, and only kept alive by machines and the incessant demands of her parents to do everything that was possible, Kerry tried to die on a daily basis.

Her parents refused to give her up, no matter how much she suffered. Their only child, they came and stayed all day, every day. They watched each action that the nurses took, monitored all the doctor's orders, demanded to know the name of all drugs and their necessity. Mr. Dawson carried around his own drug manual.

Stephanie sighed, "Her dad told me tonight that we are giving her too much sedation. He said she looks like she's dead when she's asleep."

"And yet that's the only time her tortured body can relax," Annie answered.

Kerry was six months old now. They had never been able to wean her from the respirator. A week ago, in spite of her parents' objections, the doctors had placed a tracheotomy tube to aid in her breathing. But still, she remained tied to the ventilator. Once a day, the doctors would try her off the machine for a minute or two. She could not breathe without gasping. Her whole body shook in her desperate attempts to get air.

All the nurses dreaded taking care of her, although Annie didn't mind when she wasn't in charge of the nursery. Kerry required constant attention. It took a lot of patience to sit and try to comfort her. And they had to deal with the continual questions from her father.

"She hasn't had a good day in a long time," Annie said.

"I wish she could just die," Stephanie's voice was bitter.

Annie gave her another cinnamon candy and popped one into her own mouth. "What do you think about the new ethics board the hospital is going to form?"

"I heard about it," Stephanie said. "I filled out the questionnaire that was included in my last paycheck, but I wouldn't want to have anything to do with it."

"Why not?"

"Well, it sounds like they would be playing God. Don't you think so?"

"I don't know." Annie didn't want to tell her that she had been invited to serve on the board.

"Well, I know that I couldn't do it. I shouldn't have said that I wanted Kerry to die. I always want to jump in and push more drugs when others are yelling stop. Maybe I'm afraid to let a baby die." She paused, and clicked the candy against her teeth. "My own children are so young. The thought of someone else deciding that one of them should die would drive me insane."

Annie exhaled and slumped her shoulders thinking about Kerry. How could anyone look at that little face without thinking of her agony. "I wonder if the people on the board actually get to look at the patient or do they just have the case presented and go by the medical facts?"

Stephanie glanced at the clock. Annie knew that she had already forgotten about the ethics board.

Stephanie went on talking about Kerry. "Her parents have gone for the day. They said they would think about taking her off the respirator."

Annie looked at Stephanie in shocked surprise.

"Yes, they told me that." Stephanie pulled her hair back and tightened the band around it. "The new chaplain had something to do with it. He's a sweetie, very young and soft-spoken. He's on a six-month internship from the Baptist Church across the park. He took Kerry's parents out for coffee yesterday, and apparently when they came back they asked to have a conference with the doctors tomorrow. Mr. Dawson spoke to me without his usual anger. He actually looked me in the eye, but I could tell he was very nervous."

"I've never been able to talk to him," Annie said. "He comes in and stands in the middle of the room like a big rock. I feel like I have to climb over him when I need to do something. His wife is always touching and talking to Kerry. He never touches her or talks to her. He writes in that journal after he checks the lab sheet that hangs at the bedside."

"He pats his wife on the shoulder continually when I'm taking care of her," Stephanie said. "He gives me the creeps the way he looks at me as if I am doing something wrong. Anyway, your job," and she emphasized each word slowly, "will be to keep her alive until tomorrow. Please. That's an order from Phillips. Her parents can be reached by telephone, but it'll take at least two hours for them to get here if she crashes."

Annie added this request to her growing list of problems for the day.

There was a loud burst of thunder as the rain suddenly beat against the windows.

Stephanie looked up, "It's been storming off and on tonight although it's still very hot outside."

They quickly went over the condition of the rest of the patients. Many of the infants were newly born, tiny and critical, requiring lots of complicated procedures that made their daily care tedious.

"We've got a couple of babies almost ready for discharge." Stephanie underlined their names. "These will be the easiest patients today and I've assigned them to a float pool nurse. The nursing supervisor is sending three nurses, but I don't recognize any of their names. One of them is a man."

"That'll bug the staff," Annie said. "They work hard to save these infants, and when it's time to hold them, feed them, and teach their mothers to care for them, the unit nurse suddenly has to take a new admission, and the float nurse has the fun work."

It's like nothing ever changes, she thought. Short-staffed, new doctors, storms—it seemed like she was living in a nightmare.

"I don't enjoy this kind of nursing either," Stephanie said. "It's like we are sitting on top of a bomb waiting for it to blow. All the way home I wonder if I forgot to do something that was important."

"I do the same thing, although I also worry every second while I'm here, hoping that nothing will go wrong, or that I won't make a mistake when I try to do too many things at the same time. I've had more and more nightmares lately."

Stephanie agreed. "I find myself working this place in my sleep. I can't wait until the new staff nurses pass their charge class."

They both laughed.

Annie looked over the list of nurses scheduled for the day. She stretched her arms, feeling the tired muscles already aching in her back from working the double shift the day before. "And these storms are supposed to go on all day."

"It's a test," Stephanie said, lowering her voice as the day shift nurses came through the automatic doors in a solid pack. It was exactly seven o'clock. They were chattering among themselves, smiling, eyes still heavy with sleep. A light fragrance of cologne drifted into the unit with them. They were followed by two doctors. Annie recognized the nervous blond male intern from the group she had encountered at the elevator. He was clean-shaven now and had on freshly laundered scrubs. She wondered if he would talk to her about Jessie's death.

The older woman doctor had a timid look on her tired face.

Annie wanted to welcome the doctors by saying, "Have a nice day, but please, don't do anything stupid." Instead, she simply smiled and saw a look of surprised delight cross the young intern's face as he eagerly smiled back.

Stephanie smiled at them too, and whispered to Annie, "I'm sure they've been warned that the nurses on this unit are a bunch of bitches who eat interns for breakfast."

The night ECMO nurse came into the nurses station and said, "I hate to interrupt you fine ladies, but I need to give an update before I leave this hell hole." John had a military look. Annie loved his close cropped haircut. He was older than most of the hospital techs because he had switched into nursing from a career in respiratory a couple of years ago. An excellent technician, his nursing skills superb, Annie wished he was coming on duty and not going off. His beard was bristly and his eyes had that heavy-lidded open-too-long look. The nursery was stifling now and Annie wondered if she was having a hot flash or if the air conditioner had stopped working.

"The heart-lung pump is acting up," John said.

"I didn't get to that problem yet," Stephanie said to Annie as they listened to John.

"Twice we found air in the main line. They were small bubbles, but they were visible. I was able to get them out. If air gets into that kid, it'll kill him."

Annie knew that putting a baby on the heart-lung pump was usually a last resort. It bought the baby some precious time while its own lungs could heal. They had only started the procedure recently, and it was still experimental, and quite dangerous. The surgeons had to go in and tie off a major vein—the jugular—and it would not function again normally. The baby could die in a shockingly few seconds, because they were extremely close to death when the decision was made to put them on the pump. Nobody knew yet what the long term effects of this type of treatment would be.

John sighed and said, "Phillips came in twice and brought a couple of the new interns with him. He was in his—what we call—new jolly mood and I quote: 'Do we let the baby die and not put him on the pump, or should we put him on the pump and kill him?'"

"But we've seen some dramatic results, especially in the full-term sick infants," Annie replied.

The nurses were quietly whispering among themselves in worried voices, knowing Annie was working on the assignment. Thinking about air bubbles and instant death caused Annie to shiver. She knew the heart pump had malfunctioned before. Equipment was always a problem.

John interrupted her thoughts, "For God's sake, don't let the nurses assigned to the baby leave him unattended for a second. I haven't had a break in the last four hours, haven't even had a decent drink of water." He wiped the sweat from his face.

One of the new graduate nurses spoke up, "I think you're allowed to drink water on the unit. I drink mine at the ice machine."

"I don't drink hospital water," John answered. "Who knows what bugs lurk in that ice machine. Is it ever cleaned? No, thank you."

"I don't like the taste of it," Annie said. "But I get dry working here. I've been drinking it for years and I'm still alive." Everyone grinned at her.

"You'd better jump into the shower and change your scrubs," Stephanie warned John, "or you'll not be riding home in my car." John was always fastidious in his appearance, but now he had blood stains across the top of his scrubs.

"By the way," John turned back as he headed for the lounge, yelling over the noise from the lab computer that was printing out early morning results, "don't let the neonatologist leave the unit either."

"Phillips is still on," Stephanie said. "He's in the call room."

"The blue-eyed albino," someone said in a loud whisper.

Annie whirled around in her chair. "Don't call him that." She hated that nickname. "He's not an albino. Albinos have pink eyes."

"He's growing a beard," Stephanie said.

"Is it coming in funny like his hair?" a nurse asked.

"Actually, it's almost brown," Stephanie answered. "And do you remember how he always made fun of men who had beards. He would remark that a man who grows a beard always has something to hide. My hubby said that the next time Phillips made a remark like that, I should say that I once knew a man who grew a beard all the way to the floor to hide his club foot."

Everyone laughed but Annie. She had known Phillips the longest, and Jessie's death still haunted her. He had been unusually cruel to the father and the intern, and he had hardly glanced at the dying baby. She had always admired him. And now the nurses were all talking about him. They said he was cruel, had lost his compassion, seemed distant and preoccupied.

"You two used to be quite a team," Stephanie said. "He was always respectful about my judgment, too. But last night he hardly spoke except to bark out orders. Something's happened to him. I can't figure him out."

One of the nurses spoke up. "The other day when I was helping him put in a deep-line, he told me he hated his job. He said that all we're doing in this nursery is torturing babies." The nurse had a nervous way of talking with her hands clasped together; Annie couldn't remember her name.

"He was in his prime last night," Stephanie said, as she shook off her fatigue. "He was supposed to be teaching one of the new interns, but he had him doing procedures. Then he had him running up and down the stairs from x-ray half the night. He didn't even get a chance to learn the histories of his patients."

"It's the foul language that irritates me," another nurse commented. "His vocabulary seems to have decreased, and now he only uses four-letter words."

"We don't have to listen to that," Fancy said. She was buffing her shiny nails.

Stephanie told the unit clerk that a light was out in the bathroom and turned back to Annie. "Phillips is sleeping now. He was up most of the night." A quizzical look came over her face. "One time during a code early this morning he seemed like he was physically ill. He was coughing a lot, but he said he was okay, just tired."

Annie got up. "Any more about the storms expected through the day?"

"The last update we got was that everything should be over by noon. Do you remember those wind storms we had last summer?"

"We went on emergency power."

"Well, we never knew about them until they hit. This advance warning is much better."

Annie laughed. "That's why it's fun to live in the Midwest—violent storms in the summer, ice storms in the winter. Anything will be better than this long heat wave. My grass is dead and so are my flowers."

"Has everyone noticed that the windows are all covered with adhesive tape?" someone asked.

Annie looked up and saw the tape across the windows in pod one. "Pity the poor souls who'll have to remove it." After taking a deep breath she added, "Well, all the hatches are battened down. If the windows do blow, the tape is supposed to keep them from shattering. I remember now that two windows did crack last summer. We do have a lot of windows."

"I'd sure hate to work in a room without windows," someone stated.

Annie leaned over the counter and saw that a different housekeeper was wet-mopping the hallway again. She waited while Stephanie gave some lab results over the telephone to a private physician. She noted that a portable oxygen tank was set up at every bedside in case the hospital's main line had to be shut down during the storm. The fact that the whole unit could blow up like a steam engine crossed her mind, but there was nothing she could do about that, and she let the thought go as quickly as it had come.

Annie tried to fluff up her hair and thought again about her future. *If I quit today and don't like retirement, I can always come back. I could even volunteer.* She wanted to blurt out her news and get a reaction from her co-workers. Jackson didn't know that she was turning in her resignation today. He would flip for sure. He had been after her for months. She imagined the look that would come over his face. Maybe she would tell him over the phone, if he called.

The nurses quickly wrote down their assignments. There were no complaints until Stephanie hung up the phone and said, "Happy Holiday." Only one nurse seemed completely unhappy with her assignment. She threw the assignment board back on the desk with such force that it sounded like a rifle firing. As Annie jerked her head around in fright, the nurse apologized and then pretended that it had been an accident.

One nurse said something with her back turned that Annie couldn't hear. There were the usual facetious remarks about the doubled assignments.

"Nursing on holidays has never been any fun," Annie said.

"Except at Christmas when we get a free meal," Stephanie reminded them.

Annie had assigned Kerry Dawson to Fancy. She stepped away from the desk and could see Fancy standing inside Kerry's small glassed-in isolation cubicle. Fancy was a willowy young woman, of average height, with true black hair that turned iridescent under the artificial lighting. Today she had let her long hair hang freely over her shoulders. It was freshly curled and it swung as she whirled around. Her eyes were metallic blue under her contacts, and her white skin was flawless. A small, turned-up childish nose appeared to be, perhaps, her only physical imperfection. She could eat anything she wanted, and she never gained an ounce. Everyone envied her that figure, and her lifestyle. And the fact that she was rich and didn't have to work.

Annie had once imagined herself married to a millionaire, but not to Fancy's George. She had met the man before and he was always pointing out a new watch or ring and had no words of wisdom to offer. He was unable to carry on a simple conversation. Fancy's real name was Frances, but she'd had it legally changed when her husband requested it. A month ago he had surprised her with the baby-blue Mercedes.

There was only one thing that Fancy wanted that his money couldn't buy her—her own child. She was infertile. She had spent thousands of dollars over the past three years on fertility specialists. Annie had seen her in tears so many times that she couldn't count them.

"Why don't you adopt?" Annie asked her once.

"I want a child that comes from my own body so that it will have my genes. I've felt this way my whole life. George comes from a large family. He doesn't care if we have a child or not, but he doesn't believe in adopting, either. He says it's not possible to love someone else's baby."

Annie felt much differently about loving someone else's baby. She loved all babies, but she too was childless. She remembered how Jackson used to talk about the wonder of little boys. He was fascinated with small children. When they were first married he had visited the nursery and knew immediately why Annie loved her work. They had talked about adoption more than once and had recently even talked about taking an older child from another country, but decided that it would be too much of a challenge. A friend of his had adopted two children from Russia, and quickly found out that the Russian agency had covered up some major medical problems.

Annie watched Fancy for another moment. She knew that Fancy stressed easily, even though she loved taking care of the chronic babies. She also knew that Fancy had violent mood swings. *Had she made the right decision in assigning Kerry to her?* She looked at her clipboard and looked carefully over the list of nurses. There was nobody else who would love to have Kerry.

A float nurse came up to the desk. She was furious. Her eyes glistened with anger, and her mouth was shut so tightly that her lips had disappeared. Broadshouldered like a man, tall, wearing white scrubs instead of blue ones, she had a pancake face. Her hair was pulled back severely and covered with a hairnet. She was the only nurse on duty wearing a cap. Nurses didn't have to wear caps anymore, and Annie was glad of that. A cap pinned tightly to her hair had always given her a headache, plus it got in the way when you were running around in a code.

"Mackenzie's late, as usual," the nurse said.

Overtime pay meant nothing to float nurses. Annie started to say something just as Mackenzie came running into the nursery. She was wearing a green scrub dress. Mac hated the pants suits that most of them wore. She had on real nurse's oxfords, while everyone else had switched to tennis shoes. Her white socks had lace around the tops. She was a few years younger than Annie and had worked in the hospital for many years, but had only transferred to this unit a year ago. She had been a champion swimmer in her youth, and still had the boundless energy of a teenager. She was short and square like a child's block, with rouge-dotted cheeks and happy eyes of brown. Deep laugh lines were etched at the corners of her mouth. She carried a large laundry bag full of clean baby clothes over one arm, and an over-sized brown purse over the other.

"Sorry," Mackenzie said as she paused to catch her breath. "I ran all the way up the stairs." The night nurse continued to look at her, grimly, but she calmed down immediately, even smiled, when Mac pulled a huge red apple out of her purse and handed it over. It was so shiny it looked artificial.

"I had to drop my dog off at my mother's." Her face reddened even more. "You know how scared he gets in a storm." She nodded to Annie. "His seizures have increased." She turned to the night nurse, "I'm sorry, but I have a yellow cocker spaniel named Nixon who goes nuts in a storm."

"Nixon?" the nurse replied.

"My mother calls him Jimmy Carter."

Annie laughed, explaining, "Her mother said he's not ugly enough to be a Nixon." She gave Mackenzie a quick hug.

The night nurse kept smiling but pointed to her watch. She grabbed Mac's arm and propelled her away.

. . .

The unit had quieted down as one by one the night nurses left. Annie walked over to Mac. "You have the worst assignment today," she said. "I'm sorry I had to dump on you." *It wasn't fair to dump on such a kindred spirit.*

"I saw the assignment board." Mackenzie wiped her forehead. "Whew, it doesn't look too great for anyone."

"It's 'pick on the old ones' today, but I'm so glad that you're here." Mac's smiling face, with the genuine laugh lines, was a pick-me-up for Annie.

Guy was making his respiratory rounds and he pushed a small cart of supplies into their pod. He bowed to them.

"Do you have any suggestions for our nursing shortage?" Annie asked.

"Well," he drawled like he was going to give them a serious answer, "as a matter of fact, I may be able to help you. I got a catalogue in the mail last week that you two ladies will want to see. Hospitals that are short of money, and are unable to hire real nurses, now have an option." He kept a straight face. "They can order a box of twenty disposable nurses and it's pretty cheap."

They cracked up. "You mean it's like ordering a box of rubber gloves?" Mac said. She had a cloth diaper and was wiping her red face.

"Yeah," he said. "These nurses come in three sizes," he made a circular motion with his hand. "But all of them have perfect shapes, and they are beautiful. You blow them up like a balloon. They're life-sized and they will stand at the bedside. They have a special button that you push when you ask a direct question."

Annie went along with his kidding.

Guy stood with his hands on his hips. "Well, the doctor might ask, 'What can you tell me about this patient, nurse?' Then he would push a button on her chest, and she might say, 'I don't know doctor, it's my first day in the hospital,' or 'I have never seen this patient before, before, before—'" Guy made a motion as if to whack the stuck button.

"Stop," Annie said, "I can't take anymore. I know doctors would love to push a button on our chest."

"That's not all," he went on. "If she makes the doctor mad, he could whip out a pair of scissors and jab a hole in her."

"Get back to work, before I jab a hole in you," Mackenzie said, as she pulled on a pair of rubber gloves to attend to her baby.

Annie heard laughter from the back of the nursery as she made her rounds. She headed for the ECMO pod.

Blake Clifford was the main nurse taking care of the baby. Annie liked Blake; his shy gentle ways were so different than her own. There were five male nurses in the whole hospital. Blake was the only one who liked to care for sick babies. He was slightly overweight with a large belly, but he moved gracefully on his small feet. He wore wide shoes called Earth Shoes for comfort. The father of three-year-old twins born prematurely, he often entertained the staff with their antics.

He had helped start the ECMO classes, and he knew as much as any doctor about the treatment. He trained all the new staff. Annie liked to watch how easily he handled the lines running in and out of the baby. She had not taken the classes and only knew the basics.

Annie went to sit by Libby, the nurse who would assist Blake for the day. Libby had recently come out of orientation. She was thirty-six weeks pregnant with her third child. She had fainted once, earlier in the week.

"God," Libby leaned over to whisper to Annie as she pointed to the housekeeper, an elderly black man with a goatee, who always talked to himself when he worked. "Why do they mop the floors all the time? Can't they get a life?"

"This is his life," Annie whispered back. She turned to him. "Excuse me, but when you get a chance would you move the used equipment away from the automatic doors? And please take those empty isolettes down to the lobby. Central Supply will move them from there."

He nodded, didn't look at them, and just went on mumbling.

Libby had been called in for overtime pay, and Annie knew she needed the money.

"Are you sure you can handle this assignment?"

"With Blake, certainly," she said, but Annie noticed that her eyes were puffy. She had been on duty yesterday. "Steph was worried about me too." She smiled and placed her open hands across her belly. "We both decided that I could sit down and rest more back here. My main job is documenting."

"I want you to get some juice and crackers, and put them in one of the drawers. I don't want you getting lightheaded."

"I wish this baby was more stable," Libby said. "And I pray the equipment won't act up like it did during the night shift. The baby was a little better yesterday."

Blake put down the telephone. "I just talked to baby's mama. She's pretty doped up, but all she could do was cry." He turned away, but Annie saw him wipe his eyes with his sleeve before he put on his protective eye shield.

"Just yell for one of us, or push the button when you two need help today," Annie said. "I'll sit here until you get the crackers."

She watched Libby walk away, her slender back tilted at an uncomfortable angle, her hands covering the extended abdomen. Her dark hair was plaited in a single French braid that reached almost to her waist. She had tied a scarlet ribbon at the end of the braid. She was a wonderful mother who never complained about her life.

"You know Libby has very big babies," Blake said. "The other two weighed more than ten pounds each. It's amazing she has them by natural childbirth." Blake's long cropped hair hung loosely over his ears. He had a habit of tossing it back in continual little jerks when he talked. Annie wanted to take a bobby pin and fasten the hair to the side of his head.

Tess came into the pod to talk to them. Tess was a petite redhead, and she was wearing flowered scrubs that weren't hospital issued. Her face was so pale you could see the fine blue veins in her forehead. The left side of her face was scarred from a childhood accident. The scars crinkled when she laughed, and she was always happy. She was an I'll-make-you-feel-good-or-else person. She, too, liked the chronic babies. The busier her assignment, the better she liked it.

"Hello my friends, what have you heard about these storms? It's barely raining right now."

Annie held up her hand, watching a blood pressure printout on the baby she was monitoring for Libby. She quickly recorded the numbers. "The last report I got was that the hospital is prepared. You can check the Blue Manual and go over the disaster procedures if you have time. Pass the word along, will you?"

Tess moaned. "Everyone will say they're far too busy to read anything today. Do you think Brownie, our wonderful administrator, will be here today?"

"Have you ever seen him on a holiday?" Annie said.

Libby came back with the juice and crackers, and Annie helped her hide them in the back of a linen drawer. Blake patted Libby on the shoulder. "We can do this, can't we?"

Annie headed back up the hall toward the nurses station.

A monitor alarmed and a nurse responded, "I've got it."

The hospital operator announced that the indoor celebration for the neighborhood children had been postponed.

A baby wailed thinly, wanting its mother. Annie stopped at the bedside and patted the restless form, putting the binky back into its mouth. She crooned softly to the baby until it quieted. "Hang in there. I think you're going home soon."

"Happy Fourth of July, everyone!" Annie yelled.

Nobody answered.

6:50 a.m. The Residents' Lounge

Doctor Phillips sat up in bed gasping for breath. In his dream, Jessie's father had him by the throat, and was beating his head against the wall. He shook away the nightmare. He had slept in the on-call room.

Rain thudded against the window. He got up slowly, saw the other two bunks were empty, the sheets rumpled. He was alone. The ache in his chest increased sharply when he stood. He rummaged through his pocket until he found the bottle of pain killers. He washed down two tablets with a glass of tepid water.

He showered and put on clean scrubs. He stood for a moment seeing his face in the mirror. A few days ago he had started a beard. It didn't do much for a face that was becoming more skeletal. He was a man with a terrible secret.

His doctor's words came back to him. "Cancer," he said. "It started in the prostate. The CAT scan is not good. I'm afraid it's in your lung and a rib." The man who had known him since medical school did not lie. He had maybe two months—maybe less. He was dying. He had told nobody, not even Molly, his wife.

The thoughts of the cancer and its inevitable outcome had changed his personality, sapped his strength, and killed all of his emotions but anger. Even a doctor goes through the stage of denial.

What to do? What to do? What to do?

What man ever believes he is actually going to die? How many times had he delivered a death warrant to a patient or to a patient's family?

What doctor comes to grips with the fact that he cannot cure himself? Last night he had almost collapsed in the nursery. In that instant he knew that the disease was going to win. He was sick, and he was going to die. He was forty-nine years old.

He had taken one stab at a curative treatment. One round of chemotherapy had done nothing to shrink the size of the tumors. It made him violently ill, and he was not able to work on his research. He had refused the hormone therapy that was widely recommended. He would not be turned into a woman. He had stopped the chemotherapy and started the pain killers. He tolerated the Percocet without feeling sleepy. But now, at home, he required morphine at night so he could sleep without dreaming.

I must make it through one more day, he thought.

During a Code Blue in the night, he had become weak and started to cough. Stephanie had noticed. "What's the matter? You're sick." She was an exceptional nurse, always alert in those wee morning hours. She knew something was wrong. He had recovered, mumbling something about an allergy hanging on, but he saw how she kept watching him, and he remembered how the sweat ran off his face. He knew he was taking too many pain pills. He was violent at times; he couldn't control his temper when the pain hit him with all its fury. Yesterday, one of his favorite little research pigs shied away from his touch. It was as if the pig somehow sensed the danger.

He knew he should go into the nursery, but he sat for a moment on the bunk and held his head in his hands. He felt robbed of his courage, and his research work that showed promise for the babies. He had wanted so much from life.

There was no color in his world now, none in his physical experience. Everything around him had turned to black. He had night terrors. *Was it the drugs?* He was often afraid to go to sleep. Pain sometimes kept him curled in a ball. He had major responsibilities, Molly and the girls, but he had sent them to her mother's over this holiday. He remembered the excitement in the girls as they chattered about the fun they would have with grandma, and how Molly had driven away without looking back or giving the special wave they always gave to each other. *Had she suspected something was wrong?*

He needed time to think. The pain ruled him.

Right now he was on the verge of a major breakthrough in his research. Someone else would now make known the results of all those meticulous years. The time he should have spent with his girls—all gone. *Would they remember him at all?*

He stood and looked at himself one more time, saw his darkened eyes, saw the angry lines encircling his mouth. He wanted to throw up his hands like a small boy and be comforted by someone. "Help me," he said to the room.

It would be so easy to walk out that door and keep going. For a moment he wavered. Still, some of the driving force that made him a doctor remained. He was suddenly ashamed. He went to the wall phone and got an outside line. He dialed his mother-in-law's home—the line was busy. He slammed down the receiver. It fell from the hook and dangled.

I'm on duty, he thought.

I can't walk away.

The telephone operator interrupted his thoughts. Her gravelly voice came over the loudspeaker outside his closed door. "ATTENTION, ALL HOSPITAL PERSONNEL. OUR STORM WARNINGS ARE IN EFFECT IMMEDIATELY. THERE ARE HIGH WINDS AND THE POSSIBILITY OF A TORNADO. FOLLOW THE INSTRUCTIONS IN THE BLUE MANUAL."

His beeper went off, and he quickly left the room and headed down the hall to the nursery. His right shoulder began to throb with a shooting pain. He swore softly under his breath, thinking of the cancer seedlings sprouting in his lung.

8:10 a.m. Carpenter Street

The cockroaches swarmed over the empty peanut butter jar. A table knife propped against the jar was the next victim. One shiny thick roach rode the knife to the floor as it fell. The sound vibrated in the man's ear and he rolled over in bed and untangled himself from the sheets. He was sober now, and his head felt like a block of wood on his shoulders. He reached over automatically to touch his wife's bottom, and when his groping fingers found her side of the bed empty, he remembered that she was gone. He became fully awake and searched for a cigarette on the cluttered night stand. He found one, lit it, and inhaled deeply. This brought on a coughing spasm. He looked around the room until his gaze fell upon the empty crib in the corner—and he knew he was truly alone.

The rain had let up as he flicked on the light. The crib looked ghostly. Where his baby was to have rested, there was only a box and a folded sheet. The box was filled with secondhand infant clothes and two new stuffed animals. He had painted three houses to earn money for the crib and the clothes. Jessie should be lying there, but Jessie was dead, his tiny body disposed of by the hospital with Mary's consent.

He finished the cigarette, and his head, filled with hate, began to pound. He wanted to be drunk. Alcohol, his only companion, kept the shame away. When he was drinking, he believed that nothing was ever his fault.

His wife was gone, too, because of him. Mary . . . Mary . . . she had blamed him in the end for everything—the baby coming too soon, the terrible death, the end to her world. She never said a word to him after Jessie's death. While he was in a drunken stupor, she cleared out, taking her clothes, and a few of the baby's things including the packet of memories that the hospital had given them on the day Jessie died. The packet held the blue card that welcomed Jessie into the world, a lock of hair, the patches that shielded his eyes from the lights, and a card with his footprints stamped in ink. She had written the note, and left it on the dresser.

"When you read this note, I'll be gone. Don't try to find me. My baby is dead because of you. You beat me once too often. You beat him out of me. You and the alcohol. I told Doctor Phillips about you. He was right. I should have left you long ago. I might still have my baby."

She had not bothered to sign the note, and she had done one other thing to hurt him. She had taken his dog, Trouble, a black Labrador retriever. The dog was ten years old. He had loved the dog longer than he loved Mary.

He got up from his bed. He was stiff. The finger that he burned in the middle of the night was blistered and swollen. It hurt like hell.

He was a big man, overweight from too much beer and pasta. His dirty, bushy hair was streaked with gray. He needed a bath. A man in his thirties, he looked fifty.

Suddenly, Dr Phillips face surfaced in his thoughts.

"That son-of-a-bitch won't look too good dead," he muttered, and then laughed, a bitter hacking smoker's laugh that choked him. "He won't kill any more babies."

His soul, crippled and gangrened with hate and alcohol, was inconsolable. His whole life had been nothing but pain. Alcohol kept it at bay. He had dried out three times in the past five years and Mary stayed believing he had changed. But each time he tried to start over, there was a little less of him.

He rummaged through the top drawer of the dresser until he found an old pair of scissors. A plan was beginning to form in his mind.

"I'll cut my hair and I'll shave," he said. His speech was slurred and his tongue was coated with a tobacco taste. He studied his face in the cracked mirror of the dresser. "I'll wear my glasses." He was slightly nearsighted, but he hated the nuisance of glasses and only wore them at work. The glasses would change his appearance. He would not be recognized at the hospital.

He whacked at his hair. The scissors were dull and difficult to manage with his injured finger. He tried to use his left hand, but that was awkward and the hair came off in uneven clumps.

His stomach tightened with pain and his head began to throb. He began to chant out loud. "Dead! Dead! Dead!" His voice got louder and louder until someone beat upon the connecting wall of the apartment.

"Mary," he cried, his voice breaking and hollow like that of a stranger. He put down the scissors and looked at his face, at the chopped hair, and the red-rimmed sunken eyes. His beer breath blew back into his face. He noticed the picture tucked into the corner of the mirror.

It was Jessie, taken on the night he was born.

The baby's eyes were covered with a blue pad to shield them from the harsh overhead lights. He was strapped down on the infant warming bed—tubes coming from every part of his body. His skin was wrinkled and there were visible bruises. He looked like something you find in a trash bin—a chicken carcass. He didn't look like a baby.

He took the picture, clasped it to his body, and fell backwards upon the bed. He began to pound the sheets with his fist. He pounded until his heart beat frantically and he was out of breath.

He stuffed a corner of the sheet into his mouth and sucked as he clutched the picture against his heart.

I won't cry. I won't cry. I won't cry.

He rocked back and forth.

His soul drifted further away.

8:20 a.m. The Nursery

Annie was at the desk writing down lab values on the doctor's update sheet. When a monitor alarmed, she looked up at the signal board. *Kerry's light.*

She got up quickly and ran to the baby's cubicle.

"She dropped her heart rate to forty and turned blue when I was getting her vital signs," Fancy said.

Annie barely placed a stethoscope upon Kerry's chest when the baby reacted violently. Fancy grabbed for the ambu-bag and made ready to bag-breathe the baby, as Annie yelled, "We need some help in here."

The monitor kept up the harsh sound. Mackenzie came running into the cubicle along with the new interns. The young male intern looked scared. Annie saw his hands shaking as he tried to listen to the chest sounds with his stethoscope.

Fancy waved him away. "Get Phillips," she said to Mac.

The other intern, the woman, dropped back and hung her hands just watching. Annie read the woman's mind: *Just tell me what to do.*

The puffy, pale, toad-faced infant was rigid now in a hypoxic seizure. Annie figured that her oversized lungs might have stopped. "She's shutting down."

Mackenzie said, "I've got her oxygen up to one-hundred percent." Mac disconnected the respirator and took the ambu-bag from Fancy and attached the bag to the tube in the infant's throat. Her hands were steady as she bagged, slowly in an even rhythm.

Fancy called out the necessary rate and pressure that Mac should use. They all knew that an incorrect pressure could blow a hole in the fragile, barely functioning lungs—lungs that were worn out by her premature birth and the damage caused by the respirator. On x-ray examination, Kerry had the lungs of an old man.

Annie brought the emergency drug box to the bedside. She broke the seal and began to draw up syringes with the usual drugs. She read the printed calculations on the paper hanging by the baby's crib.

The heart rate kept going down. Fancy started chest compressions. "Where the hell is Phillips?" Annie was surprised to hear Fancy swear. "You," Annie said, to the frightened intern, "start writing down the time frame on what we're doing."

The nurses worked quickly and desperately. Everything had to be documented. One of the new graduates, her eyes bright, her face frozen, was on the phone paging Phillips again. Good judgment, Annie thought. She had known what to do without being told. She would commend her later. And then, Doctor Phillips was there.

Kerry had stopped seizing and was beginning to respond to the bagging, her color now turning from cyanotic blue to pale pink.

Blue was the color of Kerry's pain.

"Damn it!" Phillips said when he saw what was going on. "Give her a dose of Valium, now."

"She had a dose about ten minutes ago," Fancy said.

"Well, give her another one."

Annie could see that he was sweating and his face looked haggard. She was shocked at how much his appearance had changed since yesterday. For the first time, she focused on the funny, scraggy beard, and thought that it did nothing for him.

"If she's still thrashing about in another fifteen minutes, repeat the dose. I want her completely out." His voice was hoarse now as he wiped the perspiration from his eyes with his arm. Everyone was sweating in the close cubicle.

Annie gave the drug as ordered, directly into the line that fed into the baby's heart.

Fancy turned to Phillips and said, "Will you write that order, please?"

Phillips ignored her. Fancy was almost in tears. Annie knew how Fancy hated confrontations. There was hostility in Phillips' voice, and she wanted to say something, but she waited to see what Fancy would do.

Phillips took over the hand-bagging for several seconds. He stared hard at the baby's face as they all watched the tortured features begin to relax. Mackenzie put a stethoscope around Phillips' neck and helped him adjust the earplugs with his free hand.

They all waited anxiously while Phillips listened to Kerry's lungs.

"Sounds like a bunch of witches cackling in there," he said, without smiling. "I think she's exchanging air now. Let's get an x-ray and see what her lungs look like." He sighed, and his shoulders slumped. He turned to the intern standing by his side and said, "Would you like to listen to her lungs, son?" This was asked in a patronizing voice.

The intern took the stethoscope and answered proudly, "Thank you, Sir. My name is Johnson, or Mark, and I only let my father call me son."

"Ah-ha," Phillips face brightened with sarcasm. "Not only is he new, but he thinks he's tough, too. Well, these gals will soon change that attitude." He bowed to the intern whose face turned a bright red.

Annie was furious at the way Phillips acted, but she kept her lips tightly clamped together. I won't confront him here, she thought.

"I'd like to listen too," the other intern said, her voice so soft Annie had to strain to hear it. She had extended her hand for the stethoscope.

Phillips glanced at her long enough to size up the teased hair and the tired face. He didn't bother to acknowledge her, and Annie watched her withdraw her hand.

The Valium was taking effect on Kerry. Her fat cheeks relaxed, and she was put back on the respirator. Her belly was blown up from the bag-breathing and Phillips saw it, too. "Open the g-tube. Get the extra air from her stomach. Don't restart her feeding for a couple of hours."

"Don't die today, Kerry," Fancy whispered as she worked with the g-tube.

Phillips must have overheard, because he turned around. "One of these times we are not going to get her back. I keep telling you girls that, so you'd better start bracing yourselves to the fact. She is going to die." There was no emotion in his voice. It was as if he didn't care one way or the other.

Annie wasn't shocked at his bluntness. He often talked in this manner. But there was something different about the way he made the statement. His face was blank, and there was not the slightest trace of compassion.

"Maybe we'd better call her parents, and tell them how unstable she is, right now," Annie said quietly, remembering how angry Kerry's father became when he wasn't informed of any changes in her condition.

"No!" Phillips spat out the word, but he didn't look at Annie. "They're off somewhere trying to make a decision about a no-code. Leave them alone." His tone was ugly. He stared hard at Kerry's lab sheet.

Annie kept her voice low and controlled, "What if she dies, and they're not here?"

He clinched his fists. "I'll take that responsibility. I'm in charge of this nursery." He then looked up, and stared her down.

He turned and started to walk away when he was suddenly seized with a coughing spell and he grabbed his head and stumbled. When he looked up and saw the alarm in Annie's eyes, he mumbled something about his allergies acting up, and left the cubicle.

Fancy went after him. "Will you please write the Valium order?" Her voice was timid.

"Take a verbal order," he said, not looking at her.

Annie was right behind him. "She can't take a verbal order on that drug," Annie reminded him. She had seen the stricken look on Fancy's face.

"Well, what the hell can she do?" His voice was nasty. Annie saw his unguarded pain. He is in pain, she thought, but from what—why?

"She can take care of Kerry, that's what she can do," Annie told him. She turned and put her arm around

Fancy and hugged her tightly. "Some of us are quite grateful that she is willing to do that today."

Phillips went down the hall to the ECMO baby.

Annie turned to Fancy. "Never mind, I'll write the verbal order myself. He can co-sign it later."

"But we aren't allowed to do that anymore. You saw the new memo." There were tears in Fancy's eyes.

"The hell with the new rules," Annie comforted her. "I can't get my work done for all the new rules. I've taken verbal orders for years. It's hard to change an old nurse's ways. Everyone knows that."

They went in to look at the sleeping Kerry. The baby lay there like she was dead, letting the respirator do all the work. "Hang on until Monday, baby," Annie said.

"Both of us swearing," Fancy whispered, "and the day barely begun."

They quickly cleaned up the clutter around the bedside, putting used needles and syringes in their proper containers.

Doctor Johnson was standing in the hallway reading a blood gas sheet for another nurse when Phillips came up to him. "Kerry is your patient today, Doctor Johnson." He pronounced the 'Johnson' with a long drawl. "You'd better stay pretty close to her room. Maybe she'll get to like the sound of your voice. Don't let her wake up." He sounded calmer and less angry. "If her nurse calls, you come running. We've got to keep her alive until tomorrow, or at least until her parents get back in town. I don't believe for one minute that they'll stay away a whole day, so don't be surprised if they show up."

Annie came up to the two doctors and handed Doctor Johnson a lab report. Doctor Johnson didn't answer Phillips, but his eyes were steady and he stood tall. Annie was proud of him. There was a new breed of doctors now. They had changed over the past couple of years. Most of them were no longer intimidated by their superiors.

And the new nurses, they weren't afraid of anyone.

Phillips started walking away and was only a few steps ahead of Annie when he sagged, turned and leaned against the wall, holding his head with the back of one hand, as he coughed.

Annie stopped. "Are you sure you're okay?" Her earlier anger had left her, and there was genuine concern in her voice. Not that long ago, he would never have raised his voice in anger toward her. They had always managed their difficulties in private.

He stared at her and there wasn't a sign of friendship on his face. He was a stranger. He spoke as if he wanted to shock her. "I'm lost," he said softly, "and the world will not find me again."

Exasperation wiped the concern from Annie's mind.

"I'm fine," he went on. "Leave me alone."

Annie turned to walk away, but changed her mind and went back to him. She took his arm and pulled him into the treatment room and shut the door.

He showed surprise at her actions. Some of his strength seemed to come back. "My, aren't we compromising ourselves, Annie?" He almost smiled and gave her a brief glimpse of the old Phillips. She had always enjoyed his humor.

"Listen," she said, "lay off the staff today, will you? They're working on overload and everyone's stressed with all these changes in the weather, and we have so many sick babies."

He stared without commenting. She felt like she was looking at a piece of stone. She put her hands on her hips as her anger built up. He was like a stranger, and everyone was starting to comment on his strange behavior. She had bowed to doctors all her professional life, but this man standing in front of her wasn't acting like a doctor.

He sighed. "Go ahead, I can see you want to tell me something."

Her voice was calm now and very strong. "I'm calling the Chief if I have any more trouble with you today."

He crossed his arms. "Who the fuck cares. Call the Chief."

Her face flamed into sudden passion. "Well, you had better fucking well care!" she said, surprising them both. She had never used that word in her life, but it felt good to say it now.

She had his attention now, and she was desperate for him to understand. She searched for the right words. "I'm sorry, I'm not myself today." She felt weepy all of a sudden and took off her glasses to swipe at her eyes. Looking around, she found a box of tissues on the counter and took one. She felt her heart racing as she blurted out the news. "Today's my last day. I'm resigning. Calling it quits. My resignation will be on the nursing manager's desk before I leave today."

"What? Why?" Now his face was the one with the question mark.

"I can't talk about it, I'm too busy. It's complicated. Please don't say anything. I haven't told anyone else. Just give me a break today. Do it for me."

He coughed and turned away as he put his hand to his mouth. "These damn allergies have gotten a lot worse." After a short pause he added, "They're going to miss you more than they will miss me."

"Why would they miss you? You're not going anywhere."

He sighed and hesitated to speak but then did. "You know what, Annie? Today's my last day, too." He gave a vicious laugh as he waited for her response.

"I don't believe you. You're kidding me, right?"

"Don't tell anyone what I've told you, please?" He almost begged. His face was anxious now, like they were in a conspiracy. His words made no sense to her at all, as she continued to stare in disbelief. Once more she saw the unguarded pain in his eyes and she knew something was very wrong. "What's wrong with you? Are you in pain?"

Someone knocked on the door and opened it. Jeffrey, the unit clerk, looked at them in surprise. "So, here you are, I've been looking for Annie everywhere. You're wanted on the phone." His young face was puzzled.

Phillips said nothing.

"Don't you say anything," Annie said to Jeffrey as they hurried up the hall. He was grinning coyly as he followed her. She hoped he would think she had been giving Phillips a dressing down. She knew the news that she was in the treatment room with the door closed would spread like wildfire through the unit. Everyone thrived on hospital gossip.

Jackson was on the phone. His loving voice calmed her nerves immediately. "Hi," he said, "I'm about a hundred miles from home."

She laughed. He had not forgotten to call. "Did you leave out plenty of food for the cat?"

"Of course! He likes me best when you're not there."

"Can't talk now," she said. The other phones were ringing.

"Love you," he said.

"Love you too," she hung up.

"What about me?" Jeffrey said, as she handed him the phone.

"Love you too," she said. He smiled. He was all of eighteen years old.

They continued to secure the nursery. Security was helping pull all the isolettes and warming beds as far away from the windows as possible, without putting a strain on the lines that connected the cumbersome equipment to the wall outlets. Thousands of dollars worth of medical equipment would be at risk during the storm, as well as the patients. And the patients could not live without their high-tech machinery.

Over the intercom Annie said, "Have sheets ready to throw over the open cribs, please." They had to protect the babies from flying glass and debris. Annie prayed they would be successful.

It was raining hard again, coming down continually across the windows. Now and then there would be the loud bang of thunder. The lights flickered occasionally, but the monitors did not falter, just hummed on.

Jack Biggs stopped by the desk. He was in charge of security. A handsome man in his early sixties, he had silver hair that was envied by all of them. It curled around his face like a woman's. Dressed in black loose-fitting scrubs, he was tall, and he walked with powerful strides. He was a mainstay in the hospital, and rarely took a day off. Everyone knew him on sight. He had a dozen children, and numerous grandchildren, and Annie knew that he played in a country band on Saturdays.

Everyone shouted a greeting as they went on with their various duties.

Biggs' booming voice filled the nursery. "I guess you folks know that the celebration in the lobby has been delayed. I am quite happy about that." He grinned.

"Yes," Annie said, "I can tell you are happy about that."

"When your parents call in to check on their babies today, ask them to stay home until these storms are over."

"Anything new about these awful storms, and when they will end?"

"There's been a lot of damage in the western part of the state," Biggs said. "I've asked the fire chief for help." There was murmuring as his words were acknowledged. "He's sending the men that he can spare. He's called in off duty firefighters. You have the sickest kids today. If we have to fall back on emergency power, I'll feel a lot better if we have the fire department's help."

Annie knew that they might have to bag-breathe by hand, and she made a mental note to give the new interns a crash course on hand-bagging the infants. She wondered if she would have enough time.

"The firemen will bring in some emergency backup generators," Biggs commented. "Just in case the main system malfunctions."

"Has that ever happened?" asked a new graduate nurse.

"Once," he said, frowning, as he remembered. He leaned back against the desk divider. Annie remembered the incident, it had happened several years ago.

"We've had a lot more trouble with power surges this summer. It's been a problem all over the city because of this continual heat wave." Biggs started to leave, but turned, and continued.

"The lobby is already filling up with people. I hope we can keep them all downstairs." The staff groaned in unison. "You folks gone over the Blue Manual?" They groaned again. "I know, I know," he said, and paused briefly, "but there might be something in it that you missed. I keep an extra copy at home—in my bathroom." There was laughter.

Guy was passing by with his cart. He stopped and spoke up. "Does the Blue Manual say anything about hidden exits? We can all escape at the last minute."

Biggs shook his head. "Stay out of the elevators if you can use the stairs for errands. Now, I have a treat for you." He opened the nursery doors, and a huge black German Shepard came in. It was Magic, the hospital guard dog and mascot. He was a magnificent animal. He stood three inches taller than a normal Shepard. His jet-black hair was beginning to turn silver around his face. He had been donated by a man who trained dogs for the blind.

Annie was thrilled to see Magic. A few days ago, Guy told her that Biggs might have to retire Magic because he was past his prime, and was having a problem with one of his hips. The board wanted Biggs to get a new dog. The big canine loved attention, but he always remained calm, and watchful, keeping his gaze on Biggs.

The hospital had taken a chance bringing the dog into the facility. However, Magic made quite a name for himself. He had been written up several times over the years in the local newspaper. He had also recently been featured on the cover of a major magazine.

Magic was allowed to roam the hospital on the days that Biggs was on duty. He was a dog with almost human qualities. He had a sixth sense about death, often appearing at a dying child's bedside without being summoned. Many a small child had passed away, safe in the arms of its mother, a hand touching the great dog's head.

Annie reached down to rub Magic's head and suddenly recalled the time he had helped calm a "crack baby" for her. The infant had been born with so many drugs in its system that it would cry nonstop for hours. It was un-calmable, even rocking did not help. Magic would come into the nursery, being drawn by the baby's cry. He would park his body by the baby's bed and utter a low moan. It drove the nursing staff wild, as the dog sounded as if in pain. But each time, after a few minutes, the baby would stop crying and sleep briefly. One day, Magic stayed all through the day shift. After that, the baby had only short crying spells.

"You're my buddy," Annie said, as she let Magic lick her face. A fretful look came over Biggs' features. "I'd like to leave him up here for awhile. He's limping pretty badly today. It's his hip."

"Leave him here," Annie said, "he can stay in the nursing station with Jeffrey."

"I'm going to retire him this week." His eyes were bright with tears as he stroked the dog's head. "I hate the idea. There are a lot of new faces in administration now. They don't know him, and they want me to get another dog." He sighed. "He's as loyal as my right arm."

"It won't be the same around here without him." Annie almost blurted out that she was leaving, but changed her mind.

"He's like an old person with arthritis in his hip. The vet said he shouldn't run at all." Biggs reached down and gave the dog a command and pointed to the desk. He thrust his fingers under the collar to make sure it wasn't too tight, and left the nursery.

Magic followed Annie into the nurses station and Jeffrey made room for the dog under the desk. Jeffrey was busy copying orders. Annie fished a cinnamon drop from her pocket, and fed it to the dog. His eyes looked tired. "You're not getting any younger, Magic. You're going to have to find greener pastures, like me." Her fatigue today was not from age, it was from indecision.

The dog finished chewing the candy, and laid his head upon his huge paws and watched her. The dog had a calming effect, and Annie slumped down on her stool while she ticked off the chores that lay ahead.

She checked on Deltiffinase and saw that Mac had changed a diaper and charted that she had repositioned the baby. *Dear Mac, she would miss her always.* No matter how heavy her assignment, she managed to do something for others.

Annie went to the first pod where Mackenzie and Fancy were looking out the window. Fancy was sucking on a piece of orange and did not bother to hide it. A fine would make no difference in Fancy's life.

The rain had temporarily stopped, but the sky was covered with dark clouds. They could see across the street into the park. The trees were motionless for the wind had stopped. There were no children playing on the playground. The giant wooden jungle gym crouched like a large insect. Annie saw the unprotected landscaped flowers, and worried about the little dogwood trees that had been planted by the Boy Scouts in the spring.

The wind suddenly picked up, and they watched the rain hit the window.

"Everything looks fried from this heat—I'm fried from this heat," Fancy said. She tried to blot her face with a tissue, but only succeeded in smearing her makeup.

"They've probably spent a fortune just keeping those flowers alive," Mackenzie said. She had her hands on her hips and looked irritated.

"I was told that the money was donated," Annie said.

"They want us to think that," Mackenzie answered. "That way, when they tell us we won't get a raise this year, we can't say that we know where the money went."

Annie shook her head in agreement. This was an annual problem. When the nurses did not get a raise, they looked around the hospital until they found something new.

The ECMO pod alarm sounded.

Annie and Mac started down the hall. "Watch the front," Annie said to Fancy.

Libby was on her knees, her great distended belly hampering her. "There's air in the line."

Doctor Phillips was there ahead of them.

Blake was on his knees also, with both hands bleeding the tubing. "Watch the blood pressure," he yelled. "I'm having problems with it, too!" Blood had spilled for a second when he changed a line. Annie saw that he had a white handkerchief knotted around his head keeping his hair out of his eyes.

Finally, Guy, who was helping by opening a packet of new tubing, nodded to Annie.

"Shit," Phillips roared, checking the pressures. "Fuck! Fuck! Fuck!" His mouth was set in a hard grim line as he tried to take deep breaths though his stopped up nose.

"Calm down," Annie said, glaring at him. "There's a parent sitting in the next pod." She could feel her pulse racing. She was not going to let this man upset her again. He was not going to change. So much for the little talk in the treatment room.

"Annie," he roared, without looking at her, "get hold of the surgeon on duty and tell him that we have to get this baby off this damn machine. Ask him to get another one ready."

Annie helped Libby to her feet, asking, "How long does it take to prime a new pump?" Libby's face was flushed with the effort.

Guy interjected, "They can prime one in twenty minutes if they can get the blood. The Blood Lab told me yesterday they had a huge reserve for the holiday. But Blair's got a two-year-old with a gunshot wound right now. He needed a lot of blood."

"How did a two-year-old get shot?" Libby asked.

"It's a sad story. Mom's a policewoman and she left the loaded gun on her bed. Her two-year-old found it while she was showering. I don't know if Blair can save the child."

"Dr Blair's on duty," Annie told Phillips, "but if he's too busy, I'm sure I can get the Rabbi. He sleeps in the hospital on holidays, even when he's not working."

"I don't know this Blair," Phillips said. "Try to get the Rabbi." He brushed past her. "I'm going down to pharmacy to fill a prescription. I'm out of allergy med."

Annie stopped him by grabbing his arm. "No, you are not leaving this unit while this baby is so unstable." She was surprisingly calm. "Write out a prescription and I'll have Jeffrey go and get it." Everyone else in the pod found something to do and left them alone.

They walked into the hallway.

He glared at her.

She didn't care. "I've got green doctors and green nurses today, and babies who are trying their best to die. You're not going anywhere."

"You always like to be the boss, don't you?" He grimaced, stopped a cough and went on. "You always want your own way." He tried to blow his nose and it seemed to take a great deal of effort. When she didn't answer, he said again, "Don't you?"

"I used to," she said. "Not anymore. I have nightmares when I leave this place." She was out of energy now and her shoulders slumped.

"I've given you a few nightmares, haven't I?" His voice was softer, in the gentle way of the old Phillips.

"That's putting it mildly, but I agree."

"Okay, chief." He bowed to her. "Forget about the drug. I'll let you be in charge. I have only one question."

"What?"

"What if I have to go to the bathroom?" He had his hands on his hips, and he was trying to smile although his face was almost gray in color.

"I'll send someone with you." They walked down the hall. She knew he was trying hard to be funny, but it was not coming off. "By the way, I don't care for that silly beard. It doesn't do anything for you."

His hand went up and rubbed his chest in a comforting manner. He knew she was closely watching his every movement. He tried to cover up with a joke. "I don't care for your red glasses either, but that won't matter to you, will it?" He went back towards the ECMO pod and she watched him walk away. He walked like he had rubber legs. There was definitely something wrong with him today. She wondered what drug he was going to get. Could allergies be making him that miserable and nasty? Was he ill?

She hurried toward the nurses station, passing a mother trying to calm her fussy baby. Annie saw the mother's frustrated tears. She was young, pale from recent childbirth, and her motions were awkward as she stroked the infant's back. The more she patted, the louder the baby cried. It was almost time for its feeding.

Annie stopped at Mackenzie's side. Mac was changing the linen on her patient's bed, carefully repositioning the tiny head. Mac gave her patients more baths than any other nurse on the unit.

Mac smiled. "My baby told me her bed was dirty and she couldn't sleep with such untidiness." Annie knew that no matter how busy Mac was, her bedsides would be immaculate before she went off duty.

"See if you can help that mother over there calm her baby," Annie whispered. "Get her to take a break and go down to the cafeteria for food. Maybe you can find time to rock the baby to sleep. You're good at it." Annie meant the praise.

"Thanks." Mac accepted the compliment. "Today I need two more arms and an extra set of legs. My feet are killing me." She reached down and straightened her lacy socks. Annie was glad she herself was not such a perfectionist. She would never get anything done. And Jackson liked a little clutter.

When Annie got to the nurses station, Jeffrey handed her the phone. It was Jackson again, which surprised her. She listened to his short concerned message. He was following the storms through news on his CB radio. "The damage is awful."

Thanks for sharing that with me, she thought. "I'm already nervous as a cow in a room full of bulls." Jackson loved to hear the old quotes made by Annie's grandfather when she was a child. "I love you," she said, "but I don't have time to talk." She paused and then blurted out, "The China trip is on."

"All right!" he said, and hung up.

He probably did not believe her. How many times had she decided she would go, and then changed her mind, saying it was not the right time? Would she still feel this way when the day was over?

She looked at the clock. "Oh my God, Jeffrey, hasn't one of the surgeons called back yet?"

"Yes . . . yes, I finally tracked down the Rabbi. Blair is still in surgery. The Rabbi has already talked to Phillips."

She sat down to rest for a moment and watched Jeffrey. He was busy setting up new charts. He was a recent high school graduate, but he had done volunteer work on her unit for the past four years. He had excellent management skills, and the hospital had hired him immediately. He was going to receive tuition help for further schooling. He wanted to be a doctor, and Annie figured he would make a good one. His short stature and scrubbed baby-faced looks made him a target for jokes. He often had trouble convincing a new doctor that he was an adult. Jeffrey was the only unit clerk she knew who never acted stressed.

Jeffrey answered the phone and acknowledged the caller. He hung up and said, "He's coming."

Mac went by and yelled to Jeffrey, "See if you can get us some free samples of Valium from the pharmacy today."

"I'll do that," he yelled back, grinning.

"Tell them to throw in enough for everyone," Annie said. "We could all use a day without worries."

Annie hurried back to the ECMO pod. Phillips was writing on the infant's chart and munching on one of Libby's crackers. He barely acknowledged Annie. He was writing with his gold pen.

"He talked to the Rabbi," Blake said. "They're priming a new pump. I just got off the phone with my wife. She wanted to tell me they spotted a tornado in a couple of places south of here, and she wanted me to come home." He grinned. "May I go?"

"Right," Libby said. "We'll just put the patient on automatic pilot and you can have the keys to my car. Did you forget that we rode in together?"

"I like your new hairstyle with the hanky," Annie said to Blake.

"I've got a devil of a headache." He frowned and rubbed his forehead. "Maintenance said they would try to find me an old fan. It's pretty hot in this pod with all the equipment."

Mackenzie came to help them change the linen under the baby because it was soiled. Annie put on a special gown, face-shield, and rubber gloves, and began to wipe the fresh blood off the base of the bed.

"Sorry about the mess," Blake apologized, "I can't keep up with this damn pump. I hope to God it will hold until they get the new one here."

"Where's housekeeping when you need them," Annie joked.

"Probably on some other unit where the nurses are running around just like we are." Libby sighed as she said, "Oh, my aching body. This kid is very active today." Annie saw the worry on her face.

Phillips looked lost in thought, and continued to tap his pen on the counter.

Since the AIDS crisis, they now looked like creatures from space. While they knew the risk of body fluid contamination was decreased with these bulky suits, it had been hard for the older nurses to adjust to all the changes. Once, good hand-washing technique had been the only major infection control.

Annie knelt down and looked closely at the lines running into the baby. She did not see any visible air bubbles. She tuned out Blake's and Phillips' conversation as she got up and scrutinized the baby lying in front of her. He lay on the elevated, large, radiant warmer, as if on a high priest's altar. The baby was swollen three times his normal size, a problem caused by the procedure. The doctors had to pump so much fluid into the baby's body, that it was hard to imagine that the grotesque-looking infant could ever return to a normal size. But they knew that the baby could improve rapidly, and quickly transform into a breathing, eating, infant with the potential to live a normal life. That was, if the procedure worked.

What an incredible pleasure it was for the staff to watch a baby, dressed in yellow or pink satin, wearing a tiny white sweater, the infant's battle scars and missing patches of hair—shaved to insert intravenous needles—hidden under a cap or bonnet, getting ready to go home. It was marvelous.

Last week, Annie had discharged an ECMO baby. He was thirteen days old and he had survived his incredible battle. Held in his mother's grateful arms, with only a small bandage visible on his neck, he had opened his eyes and stared at them with that newborn wonder that babies possess. His color was pink and beautiful and he had sucked down his bottle of milk like a trooper. The staff's only, and greatest reward, was the look of gratitude on the mother's face.

Annie checked the IV sites on the infant in front of her. He lay swollen and paralyzed by drugs, his body violated by all the artificial tubing. Let it all be worth it, she thought, as the words of the poet, Yeats, popped into her mind and she said, "*There is something about the happiness that comes from caring for children.*"

"You and your poetry," Mac said, with a frown. "I don't understand a word of it. You're the poet, so write it down for me." Mackenzie always wanted things written down so she could study and comment at a later date. Annie wrote quickly on a paper towel and handed it to Mac, who stashed it in her pocket.

"How long," Annie asked Libby, really talking to Phillips, who was sitting with his eyes shut ignoring them, "before you think this kid will be ready to come off the pump?"

Libby bent down to search the lines for air again before she spoke. "We've got at least twenty-four hours to go, unless the baby decides to cooperate and he suddenly opens up his lungs." She was helped up by Annie.

"Can you keep doing that bending all day?"

Libby was the best nurse today for this job, even pregnant, but the strain was showing on her face.

Tears filled Libby's eyes. "I sure didn't need another baby."

"Hey," Annie said, hugging her. "You'll find room for it in that big heart of yours. We all know that."

Annie walked away with Mac. "Thanks for helping everyone, Mac. See if you can get Libby to take more breaks—and Blake, too."

Blake was coming back from the bathroom. The handkerchief was wrapped tightly around his head, now. "This is my granny's trick. Just pray I'll get over this damnable headache."

"Libby's condition worries me," Annie frowned. "Tie Phillips to the chair when you need a patient-watcher, and don't let him eat all of her crackers."

"Phillips just sits there, sometimes with his eyes closed," Blake said. "Do you think he's okay?"

"I can't figure him out," Annie said.

She checked on her patient, and saw that Mac had already done her vital signs and charting.

At the desk, Annie looked at the clock as a sudden wave of fatigue came over her. She went to Mac, "Take the narcotics keys." She whipped the keys from around her neck and handed them over. "I'm leaving you in charge for a moment." She turned quickly away, not wanting to see Mac's face, for Mackenzie hated being in charge.

Annie hurried out of the unit and ran down the back stairwell, all the way to the basement. She ran past the noisy, massive air conditioning unit, and noticed two men up on a ladder working on it. She took her keycard and started to insert it in a small unmarked door, when she saw it was ajar. Suddenly, she was outside.

It was pouring down rain and the wind was blowing, but there they were, huddled under the overhang—she counted five. *Yes!* She was elated—the smokers. "Who'll give me a taste of their poison?"

Doctor Chee-Yang, the hospital's worst smoker, a tiny Chinese urologist, gave her a cigarette. He smiled at her showing his stained teeth, as he said, "I thought you quit smoking, young lady?"

"I did, yesterday," she said, "but I haven't quit yet today." He giggled, his eyes as bright as a suspicious lawyer.

The others were faces she recognized, but did not know personally, for it was a large hospital. They huddled together like condemned prisoners.

Annie sucked the nicotine into her lungs and immediately coughed. She saw it was a Camel, powerful, and unfiltered.

It was raining harder now, and the wind would gust and send a spray of water over their legs and feet. The wet air felt wonderful on Annie's face. Two more quick puffs and she put out the cigarette.

She raced up the back steps so fast she thought her lungs would burst, and knew it would serve her right for smoking. She stood still for several seconds taking great gasping breaths.

She paused outside the nursery door for a few seconds, and a moment of melancholy enveloped her. She remembered another line from Yeats, something about the evil in the crying of the wind.

Her melancholy dissolved as Phillips came out of the nursery.

"Only to the call room," he said, "don't panic." His voice sounded tired and husky. He sniffed the air. "I can't stand your perfume. It smells too much like smoke." He frowned as a strange look came over his pale face. "You got an extra one?"

"You don't smoke," she said, raising her eyebrows. "You've always been in charge of the smoke police."

"Maybe I'll start," he gave a bitter laugh. Suddenly his eyes grew moist and he looked away.

Annie thought he was going to cry after that clumsy attempt at humor. She remembered the pain she had seen in his eyes earlier. He walked on, and she remained puzzled as she went back into the nursery. She did not have the strength to take on another worry.

"I'm back," she yelled to Mackenzie. "Anything new?" she said to Jeffrey.

"Just a memo dated from two days ago, stating that there is to be no food on the units today." He paused and looked down at the can of Coke he was holding.

"Let them fire me," Annie said. "I don't care. Maybe I will join the smoke police, or the food police, or the God knows what other kind of police the administrators will come up with next."

Jeffrey leaned back on his chair and the springs creaked as he rocked. "Have you ever seen any of these groups?"

"No."

"They probably don't exist. The hospital just wants to scare us into cooperating, like that Big Brother thing in Orwell's novel, *1984*."

They both started as a giant crash of thunder sounded. They hurried to the window in the first pod. The sky had gone black, and now sheets of rain fell against the window. They couldn't see the park.

"I'll bet the smokers are inside now," Jeffrey said as he hurried away to answer the ringing phones.

Annie felt a twinge of guilt for taking her own little break. Charge nurses were not allowed outside the hospital—another rule broken, and so unlike her. Guy came up beside her. Annie punched his arm in an affectionate way. Mackenzie passed by, saluted them both, and disappeared into the cubicle to help Fancy.

"You look like you've lost your last paycheck," Annie said. "Phillips hasn't been after you, has he?" She knew Phillips hated Guy's lifestyle and took every opportunity to goad the man.

"No," Guy said, as he swallowed hard. "I just had a call from Terry. Our agent said the man withdrew from our house offer. He said it would be bad for the neighborhood to let two guys live there. He meant gays."

"Can he do that?" Annie asked. She felt a sudden stab of pain for Guy, he was always looking out for others, and it made her very sad to see him treated in such a manner.

"He did it very legally, within the time frame. He had told us what he wanted and then he raised the price by five thousand dollars." He sighed. "I can't squeeze another dollar out of my budget." He looked at her for a moment and then took a deep breath and said, "I never told you that I had a little boy."

"Little boy. You have a little boy?" He was beaming now.

"Yes. Remember when my partner died of AIDS?"

Annie remembered that sad time when Guy had taken a six-week leave of absence to care for his dying lover. He had come back to work, quiet and thinner, and it had taken him a long time to find someone else to share his life with.

"We had adopted a baby, Billy, he's now three. He's HIV positive and no family member wanted him. He had so many medical problems. He has a g-tube, but now he's learning to eat, and the drugs are really helping him. Terry loves him as much as I do. He's such a sweet kid, always laughing."

"Like you," Annie said.

"My mother has been helping with him, keeping him during the day until Terry and I get a house." He leaned his forehead against the window and sighed. Lightning was flashing continually, but the thunder was not as loud. "Man, that house would have been perfect for us. It's between both our jobs."

"That's terrible," Annie said, "and so unfair."

Jeffrey called Guy to the nurses station, and Annie followed wishing there was some way she could help Guy.

Jeffrey handed him a sheet of blood gases.

"Wow!" Guy said, "We must be doing something right."

Libby came back from a break. She had refreshed her makeup, and had put on a clean scrub top. "The light's been fixed in the bathroom." She gave Jeffrey the high-five salute. To Annie, she looked incredibly young, and didn't have the look of a mother of two—soon to be three—children.

"The firemen are coming in," Libby said. "I hope they are good looking."

"I love a man in uniform," Annie said.

"I'm in uniform," Guy laughed, twirling around to show off his scrubs.

"Great," Libby said, as she reached up and messed Guy's perfectly groomed hair. "You know we already love you."

Annie watched the two in quick, teasing banter. She breathed in the essence of the moment. The quiet joy was welcome. There was so little time for fun here. Then Libby turned at Jeffrey's remarks and ruffled his hair, too.

The three of them are so young, Annie thought. They work with a visible, cheerful sort of courage. We grow duller and tired as the years pass by. Annie felt that way today, old and tired, and even a little dull.

Jeffrey was animated as he explained the new memo to them. Every time he would say, "No food!" they would laugh out loud. Guy was leaning against the desk, his eyes bright. She couldn't see his earring, and he looked like every other man. She thought about his lousy house deal, and wished she could call up that man and curse him out. A little boy, he had a little boy.

Annie felt weary. Why, she wondered, do we have to grow old so fast? She could picture herself when she was a young nurse like Libby—see herself standing and laughing with the other young nurses. There were so many happy memories of this nursing life.

Perhaps this is what sustained her after all.

A light buzzed in the nurses station. Blake's voice came over the intercom: "I can see bubbles in the line again." They ran back into action.

9:30 a.m. The Hospital Lobby

Bobby-J paid the taxi driver and climbed out of the cab. The driver had parked under the lobby's covered driveway, and did not offer to help her with the children. She paused and waited for the automatic door to open, struggling with the fussy infant she was carrying. Behind her came a three year old boy pulling a reluctant toddler along with him.

Nineteen years old, single, and pregnant again, Bobby-J wore form-fitting red stirrup pants, and a bathing suit top. Her head throbbed from the pain of an infected tooth.

The wind blew rain against the face of the three-year-old, and he cried out at the insult. Inside the lobby, Bobby-J reached down to comfort the boy, wiped his face with her hand, and kissed his head. He stopped crying and followed her across the lobby, dragging his uncooperative brother behind him. In one corner of the room, piled high on a table, were the items that had been gathered for the children's party.

The main admission area was filled with anxious parents, visitors, and unruly children.

There were two empty infant isolettes standing along the wall beside an elevator door. There was no one at the admission desk. Bobby-J needed to find someone to hold and play with the baby. She kept patting her jaw trying to ease the toothache.

A large stuffed gorilla was propped in the admitting clerk's chair, with a note pinned to its chest: *Back in a minute.* One of the three elevators had an *OUT OF ORDER* sign posted on the door. Someone had added in marker: *Down only to the subbasement.*

Little Wayne stood beside his mother, and held on to her pants, his other hand keeping a firm grip on the shirt of Bubby, who was twenty-three months old, and missing a shoe.

The fat little baby girl in Bobby-J's arms started screaming and pulling at one ear as her tiny hands searched frantically for the pacifier that was pinned to her shirt. It dangled out of reach until her mother retrieved it, and placed the nipple into her mouth.

Over her shoulder, Bobby-J carried a large black canvas bag. The sides bulged as if they hid another child. The children were clean and healthy looking, although their clothes were a mismatch of faded colors. The baby, dimpled and blonde like Bubby, wore her hair pulled into a small knot on top of her head. A bright red bow matched the one on her mother's ponytail.

Bobby-J moaned as she sat down in the ER waiting area. She had come to have the baby's ears checked. She took a clean baby blanket from her bag, and placed it on the floor at her feet. She put the baby down and took two bottles of milk from her bag. She fished around in the bottom of the bag until she found the Infant Tylenol drops, and added some to each bottle. The baby eagerly began to suck. She handed the other bottle to Bubby, who clutched it tightly against his chest, and followed his brother over to the large fish tank that was along the wall.

Bobby-J briefly closed her eyes and rubbed her jaw near the aching tooth. She took a small pill bottle from her pocket, opened it, popped a tablet into her mouth, and swallowed it without water. A couple of older children came over and stood looking down at the sleeping infant until she shooed them away. Her boys were still standing quietly at the fish tank when she turned in her seat and glanced at the clock. She had an hour before the medical clinic opened. She had suffered all through the night with the tooth, and the pain pills barely masked the throbbing. The baby had finished its bottle and had gone to sleep.

The pain pill brought some relief to Bobby-J, and as the throbbing became a dull ache, she blinked and tried to stay awake—but she was losing the battle. She closed her eyes and immediately dozed off.

Bubby was a typical toddler, but he still loved his bottle. He sat down on the floor and began to suck down his milk, for he was bored watching the fish. He turned his head and spotted the infant isolettes along the wall. A door on the bottom of one was wide open. Bubby got up and started walking toward them.

One of the elevator lights flickered and the elevator began its decent to the basement. Ben Crock leaned against the basement wall and waited. A high school student, he was in charge of moving all equipment to the storage room, where it would be cleaned or repaired by the next shift. It was his first time on the night shift, and even though he was getting paid for working overtime, he hated it. He had spent the early morning hours listening to his Walkman, and flirting with the nurses who came to his work station when they needed a change of scrubs. He liked to engage in long conversations, and he adored hospital lingo. An irritated housekeeper had beeped him twice to remove the dirty equipment in the lobby, and he was on his way to do just that. Bubby got to them first.

The boy crawled to the open door of the isolette and climbed inside. He kicked at the door with his foot. He was a curious child. He had spent a great deal of his life in playpens and dark cribs, and he was not afraid of the dark. When he crawled into the cramped space he was still holding his bottle, laced with the Tylenol. It was soft in there, for he was lying on a piece of lamb's wool that covered the shelf. He had been up most of the night, listening to his sister cry and his mother moan with pain. He began to suck on his bottle as he closed his eyes. He was asleep in seconds.

Ben Crock got off the elevator, then reached back inside pushing the emergency stop button. He was quite muscular and wore an out-of-style Afro hairdo. He walked with a musical gate as he listened to his Walkman. He surveyed the lobby, noted the young mother asleep in her chair, the baby on the floor at her feet, the restless visitors in the seating area, and two unruly children that were going in and out of the revolving door.

There were several children standing at the fish tank. A line of parents with sick kids had started to form at the desk of the medical clinic which was now open.

Ben walked over and flipped the door shut on an isolette and rolled it onto the elevator. He then went back for the other isolette. A couple of ICU nurses got off the middle elevator. One of them, a shapely blonde, waved a friendly hand in his direction. He remembered that he had earlier given her clean scrubs.

"No more throw-ups," she yelled, making a face. He couldn't hear her words because of his headphones, but he saw her lips move and threw her a smile, flashing his gold tooth. A sweet cloud of perfume drifted his way as the nurses waltzed by. He thought of his girlfriend and the holiday meal that awaited him.

He loaded the second isolette and glanced at his watch. He would still have time to make the next bus if he hurried, that is, if they were running on time in all this stormy weather. He was calling off sick tomorrow. He was never going to work on another holiday. He closed the elevator and rode down two floors to the subbasement. The music pounded in his ears.

When Ben got to the storage room, he fished in his pocket for the keys. *Damn.* He had forgotten to get them. He tried the knob and the door was unlocked. "Sweet," he said. "Thank you my angel for looking out for me." It took Ben two minutes to transfer the isolettes to the storage room.

Bubby woke up briefly when the isolette jammed against the wall. He cried out once, then, soothed by the Tylenol laced milk, went back to sleep.

Ben never heard him, heard nothing over the sound of the music in his ears. He danced over to the wall, turned out the light, and closed the door.

He paused, remembering that the door could not be locked. But shit, he reasoned with himself. He had found it unlocked and even though he knew the hospital's strict policy about locked areas, he hesitated for only a moment. If he went back for the keys, he would miss his bus. *In this stormy weather who'd bother to check the doors today?* He was not even going to change his scrubs, and wearing them out of the hospital was not allowed either, but what the hell. He checked his back pocket and was reassured that his wallet was there.

He ran upstairs to the time clocks, clocked out, and departed through the revolving doors. The rain was coming down in force, but it felt good against his face—it had been so long since it had rained this summer. The wind had picked up and howled almost as loud as his Walkman.

As Ben stepped out from under the main lobby's overhead roof, he kicked a child's red tennis shoe from his path, and sent it flying into the storm battered flowers. He spotted the bus from a block away. It was traveling fast. He began to run.

In the lobby, pain jolted Bobby-J awake. She sat up and rubbed her throbbing jaw. All the seats were now filled with parents and crying children. Someone was listening to a weather report on a small radio. Bobby-J began to whimper and looked down at her sleeping baby. The baby had its thumb in its mouth, and had rolled partly off the blanket. Bobby-J turned her head and searched the lobby for her boys. Little Wayne was still at the fish tank.

She scanned the lobby for Bubby, but he was nowhere to be seen. She panicked, jumped up and scanned the area again.

There were several families in the area waiting to be admitted. None of the children looked like Bubby. She saw a security guard talking to a fireman. There was an elderly man standing at the volunteer's desk, crying and holding a sack of children's toys. There was a taxi driver talking on the telephone. But there was no Bubby.

The rain was coming down in sheets against the only large window in the lobby. It was black outside and all the lights were on in the lobby. Bobby-J got down on her knees and began to search under every seat. She knew that Bubby liked to crawl into dark spaces.

She crawled up to the broken, string-tied shoes of a homeless man. She knew him as "Jolly," and had given him small change before. He was often there in the lobby, sitting for an hour or two, and all the staff knew him. He sat—asleep—with his hands folded, protecting a large torn shopping bag. She crawled around the legs of a teenage boy, sitting in a wheelchair, and received a sharp rebuke from his mother.

No Bubby!

A scream tore from her throat: "Bubby! Bubby!" She grabbed her baby and ran toward the security guard.

Jack Biggs turned, startled at the high shrill screams. He automatically reached down and held securely to Magic's collar. The big dog had just been brought down from the nursery.

. . .

Upstairs in the nursery, Annie was listening to the news on Jeffrey's portable radio.

Doctor Rustov, the chief surgical resident, known as the Rabbi, came into the nursery.

He was a small thin man, wearing a black silk cap that covered his entire head. The cap protected his scalp, scarred from a childhood fire that had killed his parents and siblings. His black eyes dominated his face when he smiled—and he smiled a lot. "I smile," he would say, "because I believe that everyone should be smiling in a children's hospital. If you can't give these little ones some joy, you shouldn't be here."

Annie loved the mysterious element of the surgeons' world. She sensed that theirs was a lonely glory. They had to conquer death in such frightening ways. Most of the surgeons she had encountered, even the women, were often harsh and unfriendly. *Too serious.* Annie had seen some act like they were God.

Doctor Rustov was different. He was a splendid human being. She had never heard him raise his voice in anger. She had seen him openly weep at the death of a child. He spent as much time as possible with parents explaining procedures, and was usually the first person out of the operating room to speak to the patient's family. He never dabbled in politics or hospital problems. "Politics can go either way," he was prone to saying. "They make no difference to me. The child is my only interest."

He appeared on the evening news, occasionally. He would talk about safety and the need for car seats. He was recently promoting helmets for skateboarders.

He had come into the nursery to answer a page. Annie dialed the number he repeated to her, and handed him the phone. He frowned, letting his tired eyes blink shut as he talked.

Annie knew that he was almost finished with his residency, and in another few days he would be gone. She looked at his hands as he talked. They were small and delicate, and covered with fine silvery-white scars. He had been burned over eighty percent of his body, but his hands were fully functional.

When the Rabbi hung up the phone, Annie offered him a paper cup filled with ice water. He took a cinnamon drop from her, and stuffed it into the pocket of his scrubs. "For Max," he said, grinning. "He'll be here soon. I'll just rest for a moment"

Jeffrey scrambled out of his chair.

"Ah, not your seat, child," the Rabbi said.

Annie laughed when she saw that Jeffrey took the remark in stride, his boyish face twisting into a grin. "I have to make a trip to the lab, anyway," Jeffrey responded.

The Rabbi sat.

"How's the gunshot victim?" Annie asked.

A shadow crossed his features as he sipped his water. He sat the cup down, and looked at her for several seconds before he spoke. "His brain is dead. The machines are keeping him alive. That call was from Blair. He wants me to see if the mother is able to talk yet about organ donation." He bent forward and rested his head in his hands.

"Ah, that mother—one careless mistake." He brought his hands together, the delicate tips of the scarred fingers touched. "She's a policewoman—worked a double shift yesterday. Just laid that gun on the bed without thinking. She heard it go off."

Annie winced as she imagined the sound of the gun.

"She hasn't left that child's bedside," he said, shaking his head. "She's got blood all over her clothes, and the nurses could only put a gown over them. She keeps hold of the baby's hand. Half the nurses are in tears, and now we've got another trauma coming in."

"Is it bad?" Annie didn't want the answer.

"Kid thrown from a moving car—no car seat. Oh, when will they learn?" An audible touch of pain was in his voice.

Annie said nothing.

"You know, Annie, I wish there were no guns."
He sighed and took a deep breath and was lost in
thought.

"We don't allow any in our home," she said.

"I hunted when I was a child," He looked at her
with a steady gaze as he remembered. "The first time
the animal went down—it was a big buck, my grandfather shot it—that was enough for me." He cringed as
he recalled the event. "I can still see that magnificent
body, the huge antlers. I looked into the startled eyes
before it fell."

Annie nodded. "When I was a girl, my father took
me rabbit hunting. He would kneel down and aim that
rifle, but he never even hit one. I don't think he in-
tended to. I think he just thought, since he was a man,
he was supposed to go hunting."

Annie suddenly wanted to know more about the
Rabbi. "Where will you go from here?"

"Why Annie, I'm glad you asked. We're going back
to Israel. My wife misses the Holy Land and we want
Max to grow up there."

"We will miss you here—on this holy ground," she
said.

"You'll have Doctor Blair. They say he was here as a
resident, and that he was well respected by everyone."

"Yes, he was here, long ago, but I know him."

"Say, Annie, do you remember my first Fourth of
July and what happened on that day?"

"You mean that teenager who had been shot,
and dumped out of the car on the front lawn of the
hospital?"

"What a nightmare. And you, my dear Annie, you
ran that code in the lobby."

"We were lucky with that gunshot wound, weren't we?" He smiled as he remembered.

. . .

The automatic doors opened, and they both heard the excited voice of a small child. "Is my daddy here?"

The Rabbi jumped up, his face alive with joy. "Max," he cried. He limped a little as he hurried to meet the child—another reminder of his long ago accident. But he was even graceful when he limped. He swung the child up into his arms, and they waved as they left the nursery.

He will take so much color with him when he leaves, Annie thought. His kind always does. *Where do people like him come from?*

She suddenly thought about Blair, remembering when he, too, was a struggling resident. How hard he had worked. She hoped another resident would come along this year, who would make a difference like these two had. It was a comforting thought.

Annie wanted to believe they would miss her presence in the nursery, but she preferred to envision someone taking her place. I am getting ready to leave here, but hopefully somewhere in the city, a person is deciding to become a nurse for these tiny babies, she thought. She pictured someone filling out the application.

The telephone began to ring almost constantly, with worried parents, unable to visit, concerned about the safety of their babies.

Everywhere that Annie looked, there was a receiver off the hook. For some reason, the calls would not transfer, forcing Jeffrey to run up and down searching for caregivers. Doctor Phillips then came in, parked himself in a corner of the nurses station, and tied up another phone.

At least he had calmed down a little, Annie thought, but he still looked pale and distraught. The interns were bringing him problems, and for once, he seemed to be patient with his replies. To Annie, this was an improvement over his snapping and snarling like a mad dog.

Guy arrived with a set of blood gas results on the ECMO baby. Annie saw Phillips look long and hard at the young man. He said nothing, as he jotted down new orders on the sheet. When Guy left, Phillips raised his head and said very sweetly, "The Gay Prince Charming of the Fairy Story."

Annie ignored the remark and dialed the nursing office. Three ill calls had already come in for the night shift. She thought that two of the calls were probably weather related, as those nurses lived far from the hospital.

"Nursing office . . ."

The gravelly voice brought a grin to Annie's face.

"Barker in the NICU, Maggie. I guess all the old folks are working today."

Maggie laughed in that full-throated laugh of a chain-smoker and said, "These new doctors. One couldn't remember the combination to his locker, and I had to have security cut the lock off."

"I've forgotten mine before, and once after a long vacation," Annie said.

"But not on your first day, right? I've had one gal faint in surgery. Turns out she's pregnant, but didn't want it known yet."

"It won't be a secret now," Annie chuckled.

"One of the med-students had a grand mal seizure up on the sixth floor. He had forgotten to take his medication." Maggie paused for a coughing spell.

"Sounds like you could use an assistant."

"I wonder, if a doctor can't remember to take his own medicine, how in the world can I trust him with a patient?" Maggie sighed deeply. "And all I hear about is the threat of a damn tornado."

"We'd better not get a tornado," Annie said. Jesus, she thought, that is the last thing we need today. "Mac's working too, and her dog has seizures during storms, so it's on medication."

"Seizure medication for a dog?" Maggie laughed. "I am too damn old for this job."

"The nicest thing about growing old, Maggie, is that you get to do what you want?"

"That's a damn lie, Annie. I would be parked on my sofa, with a bottle of champagne, instead of stuck in this office. Run down if you get a chance, my sister baked me a pan of fudge, and I'll share. I don't need all these extra calories, but it's damn good."

"We can't eat up here," Annie said, noting that Jeffrey was chewing on something.

"I hope you're not calling for extra nurses, because I sure as hell don't have any. What I could use right now is a cigarette."

Annie remembered that Maggie had gone cold turkey off smoking, after she had suffered a major heart attack in the spring. Still, the tough old army nurse craved her nicotine. She had come back to work a shadow of her former self, and all that lovely black hair had gone completely white.

"I don't know how we'll do it," Annie said—she wouldn't beg.

There was a long silence, and then Maggie sighed. She was a sucker for the NICU. "I'll call the agency. I'm sure someone will come in for triple pay."

This made Annie furious and she spouted off, "My nurses would gladly come in for triple pay, even double pay, but nobody offers it to them."

"Now, Annie," Maggie tried to calm her, "you know how the administration feels about double pay."

"Sure," Annie fumed, "and where do you think the administrators are today? Do you think they are around here?" Maggie tried to speak, but Annie was on a rampage. "Don't send me any dregs of humanity." She knew she would have to take any nurse she could get, but she added, "Make sure they know how to take care of babies. I won't have any mistakes today."

"Annie, I understand."

"And one more thing, Maggie."

"Yes?"

"Tell them that the charge nurse is a real witch. I'll be the one wearing the tall black hat."

Jeffrey came into the unit carrying a can of diet pop. Annie grabbed it, and poured some into a paper cup. She drank it down quickly. It burned her throat and tasted delicious.

Jeffrey handed a phone to Annie. It was Heather, with a transport. Annie could barely hear her over the static on the line. "We have a preemie, born in a wreck, he's bad." The call dropped, and the phone rang again—it was Biggs.

"Annie, the team is five minutes out. Are you ready for them?"

She flipped the intercom. "A transport is coming in five minutes, very bad. Anyone with a free hand, please check the admission spot to see if it's ready."

She asked Biggs, "Any history?"

"The mother died. Even in this heat, they haven't been able to get the baby warmed up. He may not make it to the unit." He said something else with the mouthpiece covered. Annie heard a woman's panicked voice talking to Biggs. "Shit," he said, to Annie, "I've got to go, I've got another problem." He hung up.

'He,' Annie thought. The baby born in the wreck was a boy. She went to find Phillips, who was explaining an x-ray to a red-faced, quiet Doctor Johnson. She hoped they had not gotten into it again. She interrupted, "Transport's coming in. A preemie, and bad."

Phillips had combed his hair flat, and it was wet. He had changed into clean scrubs. His face looked drawn, and Annie realized for the first time that he was much thinner. He looks like an old man today, she thought. He's at least five years younger than I am. *What's going on here?* He glanced up, and she saw the raw pain in his eyes—but she had no time to think about Phillips. She hurried back to pod one. She would have to admit this baby.

Annie quickly checked over the supplies. Everything was in order. Mac had moved the scale next to the warming bed, and there was a warming light ready to turn on.

"I did your check on Del-baby," Mac yelled.

"I owe you a lot, lady," Annie yelled back.

"Put it on my tab."

Phillips was standing by the window and holding tightly to his shoulders. His back was stooped. The wind was roaring so loudly, they could no longer hear the thunder. They waited.

The phone rang.

"Still five minutes out," Jeffrey yelled.

The five minutes passed. She watched Phillips, discreetly. He had real concern etched on his face. This was the man she had known for so many years. Somehow, over the past few weeks, he had become a monster, terrorizing the nurses, abusing the house staff, screaming at his wife on the phone. Each time Annie came on duty, someone had a new horror story.

Jessie's death scene replayed in her thoughts. Phillips had come to the code late. She did not want to believe it had been deliberate—but she was not certain.

Phillips had argued with Jessie's father each time he visited. How upset the man had gotten when Phillips told him there was little hope. The baby had suffered another bleed into his brain.

"He ain't dyin'," the father said. Phillips had not answered him.

And there had been the time when both parents were out of the room, and Phillips said to her, "That man doesn't deserve to be a father. His actions brought about this premature birth."

"Don't let him get to you," she replied. She had added, "We have fathers like this all the time. It's not our place to judge him. Let the courts take care of him."

She remembered that Mary had indicated that she was going to file an abuse case against the father, and had done so on previous occasions.

Phillips had expressed his disgust. "Look at Mary, she hasn't a clue as to how really evil that man is. I smell alcohol on him, and he denies he's been drinking."

As a monitor alarmed, Annie shook away the thoughts. One of the preemies had 'decided' not to breathe, and had dropped his heart rate. She quickly opened the door of his isolette, flipped his foot, turned him over, and repositioned the plastic oxygen tube that had slipped from his nose. The baby immediately pinked up in color, and let out a wail. She patted him until he was calm.

She quickly washed her hands, noting that Phillips still stood at the window. Although he had not turned to watch, she could tell by his apprehensive manner, that he had been listening.

"Why isn't that transport here?" he said.

She wondered . . . what if she just walked over to him now, and asked about Jessie's death? *Did he want Jessie to die? Did he really try to save him?* She had to know.

Guy came running into the pod with a clean respirator. He flashed his irresistible grin. Annie's heart softened, and her thoughts turned away from Phillips. Guy had a vast tenderness for people, especially young people. He was always the first person to introduce himself to the new staff. She had watched him welcome the new interns today, and praise them. Last evening, he had 'loaned' away all his money, and when they got to the cafeteria, he had empty pockets. "No money," he had said, "but who needs it?"

"Well, it can buy your dinner," Annie had retorted wryly, forcing him to take a couple of dollars.

"Can it buy back one of our baby's lives?"

"Can it keep people I love from dying of AIDS?"

As she now watched Guy set up the respirator, she wondered if he had heard any more about the house contract. She had a little money stashed away for emergencies, a small inheritance from a distant childless aunt. Maybe she could find a way to offer him a loan, she thought.

Guy was humming softly to himself, *Yankee Doodle.* Annie joined in. After all, it was the Fourth of July.

• • •

The doors swung open and the baby was there. A tiny boy—blue and gasping for breath—his body buried in a mass of wires and plastic tubes. He was lifted out of the travel isolette, quickly weighed, and placed on the warming bed.

"He was intubated," Heather said, a tiny redhead in charge of the transport team, "but it came out in the elevator."

"He's so blue," Annie cried, noting that his skin was bruised and even bleeding in places.

Phillips began yelling out orders. He got the indotracheal tube into the tiny lungs on the first try. Annie took over the bag-breathing, noting that Phillips face was covered in perspiration, and as white as the wall behind him. His hair was now soaking wet, and he kept swiping at his face with his arm.

Guy pumped the tiny chest, as fragile as an eggshell, trying to keep a walnut-sized heart beating. Annie hooked the baby to the wall monitor. The heart rate hovered below sixty.

"Baby, don't die!" Annie was frantic, feeling her own heart speed up.

Mackenzie wrote everything down, calling out the heart rate every minute, as she recorded every action, every drug pushed.

Phillips gave three rounds of drugs.

"I can't get a blood pressure," Annie said.

They worked for several more minutes. Then Phillips raised his hand to stop the action. Someone called out the time of death. There was only the high-pitched scream of the wind, and the rain beating against the window.

But there would be no time to contemplate the death of this tiny boy.

"I need help—now!" Fancy called out, and everyone rushed to Kerry's room.

Annie stayed with her baby. She closed the sightless eyes, and gently removed the tubing and monitor leads from the battered body. She felt the baby's warmth slipping away.

Mac came back to help. "Kerry's stable, now," she whispered. Annie bathed the baby with warm cotton balls. She looked at Mackenzie, and saw that her eyes were wet.

Annie wrapped the perfectly formed body in a new, soft, blue blanket. She had blood on her hand from his bruising. She carried him into the treatment room. She stood there thinking about his mother—dead at the scene.

She wondered about the father. Where was he, would he come? *Would anyone come?*

All she knew about this baby was written on the plastic band around his ankle: *Baby Boy James.* This was his life. *Who will weep for him?*

She held the tiny bundled body against her chest—close to her own heart—his blood drying on her hand.

"Someone will take you back to your mother," she whispered, as she laid the lifeless boy on the cold, sheet-covered hospital cart. The room, full of medical equipment, a fuzzy grinning bear on the wall, was no place to leave such a tiny boy.

Someone called her name. The voice was urgent. Annie closed the door, then opened it, and turned on the light—not wanting to leave him alone in the dark.

11:04 a.m. The Nursery

The telephone operator's voice came over the loudspeaker: *ATTENTION ALL HOSPITAL PERSONNEL. CODE RED A. CODE RED A.*

"What the hell's a Code Red A?" Phillips had come up behind Annie. She had just finished a check on Del-baby, and was at the desk wiping her face with a cloth diaper. She stopped and they both listened as the call was repeated.

"A Code Red is a missing child," Annie said. They went to the Blue Manual and looked up the code suffix. "A Red-A means a child is missing somewhere in the hospital, but it isn't a patient. Maybe that's what Biggs was talking about when he said he had problems."

"My God," said Phillips. "We don't need this."

Annie remembered an incident that had happened last summer. A baby was snatched from one of the upper floors by a woman who was later declared to be mentally incompetent. The woman had taken the child from a room, and was seen by a housekeeper. She had put the baby into a hospital stroller, and wheeled it right out the front door. When the baby's mother returned a few minutes later, they issued the Code Red. The police had found the baby, unharmed, six hours later. The kidnapper had taken it to a supermarket and was buying baby things. An alert cashier noticed the needle marks on the baby's head.

"Hey, Jeffrey," Phillips yelled toward the nurses station. "Find out the details about this missing kid?" Phillips took a bottle from his pocket and popped a couple of pills.

"Don't you need some water to drink with those?" Annie asked. They went to the water fountain where he took the cup of water she offered. He put his hand to his forehead and rubbed it vigorously.

Annie went over to the window in the first pod. "You can't see the park. My grandpa used to say, 'It's so dark, it's as black as the devil's heart.'" The wind whistled around the edges of the window. Tiny white balls of hail were collecting in the corners. "How in the hell can anyone let go of a kid on a day like this?" Phillips said behind her. Annie didn't want to think about it.

Five firemen came into the nursery, followed by Biggs and two other security officers. The firemen carried their heavy equipment like it was made of Styrofoam. Biggs and his men rolled in two large portable generators. Magic limped in behind them, his coat wet from the outdoors. Magic was happy to go back to the nurses station, where he went under the desk and began to groom.

"He's very nervous," Biggs said, his gaze following Magic. "Dogs hate storms. He won't be in your way, will he?"

"He keeps me calm," Annie said, following the dog into the station.

She felt she could relax a little, now that the firemen were there. They took off their heavy yellow raincoats, but kept their boots on. They were extremely big men, dressed neatly in blue uniforms, their names stitched over the pockets. Two nurses came to greet them.

Biggs asked for everyone's attention. "We've got another problem. The storm is supposed to be the strongest in the next couple of hours. The highway patrol reported that it's shifted a little, and may take longer to get here, but there ain't no way in hell it's gonna miss us." He looked at a pad in his hand. "You've all heard about the missing kid by now." There was murmuring on the unit.

"It's a strange situation. There's a young mother down in the emergency room being treated for an abscessed tooth. She was up all night with pain. She brought her baby in to the medical clinic. She had two other children with her. She was waiting for the clinic to open, and fell asleep in the lobby. When she woke, her twenty-three month old boy, named Brick—she calls him Bubby—was missing. I thought we'd find him immediately, maybe outside the hospital. We checked with the grandmother, who confirmed that he was with the mother. We found one of his shoes in the flower bed outside the lobby doors, but the mother said he had lost it on the way in, because she remembered he was only wearing one shoe in the lobby."

"Did she check in, when she came into the lobby?" Annie asked.

"She said there was nobody at the desk. She said the boy wouldn't leave the lobby by himself, he's too small, but later she admitted that he wanders off." There were short whispered remarks among the staff.

"I've got a guard or volunteer posted on every floor. The city police are here now. The first search turned up nothing. The lobby is full of parents with sick kids, but people don't remember that kid. They remember the mother, and the baby, and the older boy who hung around the fish tank." He paused and wiped his brow. "You want to believe that he's just wandered off, but where? I think someone must have him."

"I hope you find him," Phillips said in a hoarse voice, "but we haven't seen him, and we have too many other problems to worry about."

A city policeman came in, and he and Biggs left together.

Kerry's alarm rang again, and Annie went to her cubicle. Fancy had tears in her eyes, and stress written all over her face. "It's not going well," she said.

"Go take a break, I'll sit here." Annie gave Fancy a hug. "What a heck of a holiday we're having."

Fancy blew her nose, and washed her hands. When she turned from the sink, she was grinning. "And would you believe that George called and wanted to know why I hadn't rented him any movies? He said I knew the storms were coming, and he wouldn't be able to go fishing."

"I didn't know anyone still went fishing. I thought all men played golf, or watched football or something."

"Does Jackson play golf?"

"He tries to. Most of the time he just polishes his clubs and says he's going to play—one of these days."

After Fancy had gone, Annie turned to Kerry. The baby was quiet, and her eyes were closed. Annie took a seat on the high-backed stool beside the crib. She tried to prop her feet on the crossbar, but they kept slipping off.

She watched Kerry. The baby was letting the respirator do all her breathing. It was obvious she was sedated. Her fat cheeks showed the effects of the massive steroids she had been given to keep her alive—if one could call this living, Annie thought.

The baby was ugly. She puffed her cheeks with each breath, and looked like a giant toad. Her ventilator pressure was way too high for her age. Her damaged lungs were like rubber, and hard to inflate. Her belly was still distended from the earlier code. She looked like something from an alien movie.

Kerry's arms and legs were pencil-thin. It was impossible to nourish her properly, although a nutritionist visited daily to adjust the caloric level of her formula. Her feeding tube snaked from her stomach, and was suspended on a string that hung across her crib. Milk dripped at a constant rate, and if she fussed, it backed up and overflowed the syringe. It was extremely hard to keep her bedding clean, and there was always a sour, gastric smell.

She could not tolerate normal feedings. She vomited frequently and lost weight. She had never had a bottle in her mouth, or tasted her mother's milk. Sometimes she would suck on a special vanilla-flavored pacifier for comfort.

Around Kerry's crib were all the signs of a normal baby: a music box that played '*It's a Small World,*' a string of brightly colored rattles, a stuffed Mickey Mouse—eyes open, mouth fixed in a happy smile.

Children's books were piled high on a bedside stand. On the counter sat a box of cards from a grandmother far away in Alaska. A stuffed dog—pen around its neck—invited doctors and nurses to sign their autographs. A picture of happy parents in wedding clothes was taped to the crib at eye level. Under the crib was a decorated clothes basket filled with stuffed animals, and little pink dresses—never worn.

A fluffy pink blanket was draped over the crib to shield her eyes from constant, harsh florescent lights. A monitor lead wrapped around her toe, to register the oxygen concentration in her blood. When it alarmed, the numbers danced up and down to warn the staff. Every day of her six months of life, she had been unstable, and 'trying to die.' The nurses all believed this.

Kerry was too sick to dress and cuddle. Her parents had to settle for holding her hand or touching her face, and only then if she tolerated the touch.

During rounds that morning, Phillips had commented to the new interns: "Here's a face that only a mother could love." Yet, there were times when Kerry was calm, and you caught a glimpse of the real person she was trying to be. During those few minutes, when she was not gasping for breath, she would stare at you, her bright blue eyes filled with questions.

Her mother, Addy, would sit for hours at Kerry's bedside, talking to her, reading to her, and holding her hand. Kerry would work her mouth around the fat-nipple pacifier, and suck as if eating. Once, her mother had called Annie to the bedside. "Look," she said, her face glowing with maternal pride, "she's trying to tell me something, don't you think?" Later that day, Annie saw the inconsolable sadness on Addy's face—like the face of a priest giving Last Rites.

Annie remembered that day, looking down at Kerry's searching eyes, the busy mouth, the tiny hand clutching a mother's thumb. She had left the room defeated, with a terrible feeling that the baby did, indeed, know what was being done to her. Kerry brought Annie down to earth—made her feel evil at times. *What would an ethics board say about the life that Kerry was forced to live?*

There were days when Annie could feel Kerry's family being destroyed. The father standing at the bedside, his face cold and sullen, speaking only to his wife, busying himself with details, noting every change that the doctors ordered.

Annie knew that Kerry was dying. The doctors were no longer as aggressive with her treatment. The x-rays showed the enlarged, crowded heart that filled her chest. They showed the lack of bone growth, the tiny fractures in her ribs. The doctors and nurses argued every day.

"What are we doing for this baby?" her primary nurse asked two days ago. "I can't stand to watch her breathe," said a lab tech, trying to squeeze blood out of Kerry's heel. "But it's our job," a med-student commented. "We can't just kill her." He had laughed nervously, but nobody joined in. The doctors were always eager to leave Kerry's cubicle.

Annie spoke in a normal voice that day. "Why don't you stand at her bedside for twelve hours?" They could hear the bitterness in her words. "You doctors come in only when we have a crisis. You aren't the ones who have to coax her to breathe."

"You don't have to stick her bruised heel, three times a day, for a blood test," the lab tech interjected, as she finally finished her task. A student nurse added rather timidly, "Or keep her occupied for hours, so she won't vomit."

"Every day, a needle stick in that tiny heel," Annie said, "and we have to watch her mother cry."

The doctors had fallen silent, even Phillips had pursed his lips into a tight line. The resident flushed in embarrassment. He was only cross-covering, and her condition was not his doing.

They quickly shuffled away and Kerry was forgotten. And here she lay, still struggling.

Annie remembered another night. Kerry's mother was very late arriving at the hospital. Her car had broken down, and she finally arrived by taxi. She couldn't bear to let a single day pass without visiting Kerry. Kerry was her whole life.

Annie had been her nurse that evening, and was at the bedside doing last minute charting. Kerry had already coded two times. Her color had been blue most of the shift, and she had required a lot of sedation.

Addy had leaned over the child, and lifted the frail little hand. She touched the hand to her cheek, and then lost control and wept. Kerry began to stir, hearing her mother's sobbing, and was soon gasping for air. Addy continued to weep, while Annie was forced to sedate Kerry for a third time.

"I was so healthy," she told Annie. "I did everything right. I ate . . . slept . . . lived only for her. I've waited so long to hold her. It's hard . . ."

Annie had put her arms around the young mother, shocked at her terrible thinness. Annie felt as if she was holding another child. Addy was only twenty.

"I can't let her go," Addy said, repeatedly.

There was no relief for the baby—none for the mother—none for the staff.

12:00 p.m. The Convenience Store

STOP AND SHOP, the sign read in bold yellow letters. Below, printed by hand: *If You Can't Find It Here – You Don't Need It.*

The man placed his purchases on the counter, and reached out to pet an ancient fat calico cat, that was cleaning its face with a crippled paw. The cat hissed and leaped from the counter, disappearing behind a cereal display in the main aisle.

It was not his neighborhood. The clerk was a gum-cracking, middle-aged woman, with gray hair clipped short, and pinned behind her ears. She had her back to him, watching the news on a small color television mounted on the wall. She held a battered paperback in one hand.

The newscaster was speaking in a monotone: "The rain is heavy . . . winds are strong . . . reports of flash flooding . . . possible tornado in the western part of the county . . . some sections of the interstate are closed . . . a child is missing . . . stay tuned . . ."

"I'm ready," the man said, as thunder crashed, and wind beat the rain against the door. He was dripping wet. He gestured toward his things: a six pack of beer, three ready-made sandwiches, two packs of cigarettes, and a bag of chips.

The clerk turned, and without looking at him, began to ring up his purchases. She wore rimless glasses, spotted with grime, which sat crookedly on her nose. She had a look of monotony on her face.

He raised his right hand, and pointed the black, shiny revolver directly at her. "Think this will cover it?" He cackled at his joke.

She jumped back instinctively, her eyes fearful and alert. She looked directly into his face, and saw eyes full of anger and secrecy. She noted the chapped, razor-scraped face, chopped hair, black framed glasses, and the sharp nose. A deep frown puckered the man's forehead. His sickly skin had the fading color that identified a drunk who spent too much time indoors.

She continued to back away until she was against the wall. It felt solid against her blue smock, and it strangely comforted her. Her knees were shaking and she thought she might fall. She threw up her hands and said, "Take it." For a moment, she considered moving her foot toward the alarm on the floor, but quickly abandoned the idea. She had been robbed before, and she was not a hero.

She closed her eyes and waited. The news drummed in her ears: *Stay inside . . . trees are down . . .* She thought of her husband's words: "Never look a thief in the eyes—it makes them nervous." She could hear the roar of her heartbeat. *Please don't shoot me. Please don't shoot.* The words galloped in her head.

She heard the rattle of a package . . . something hitting the floor . . . a muttered curse. Then a crash, as the man kicked a display. She heard the howling of the wind as the door opened, then the door slammed shut. She waited, as her heartbeat slowed. For one crazy moment, she thought it might stop altogether.

She stumbled to the door, locked it, put the closed sign in place, and pulled the blind. She slowly went behind the counter, and pushed the button on the phone which dialed the police. Only then did she collapse on the floor.

"I've been robbed," she yelled into the phone, and remembered that the man had not taken any money.

"Lady, are you in danger?" a young man's voice inquired.

"Not now. He's gone. But I might have a heart attack."

"Stay on the line. Someone will take your information. We can't send a patrol out in this storm unless your life is in danger."

Her hands still trembled. *They would ask for a description.* She remembered that the man was wearing a cheap plastic raincoat, like the one she bought at the state fair. She reached up to the counter and found her cigarettes. Her cat climbed into her lap and began to lick her face, purring loudly. She hugged the warm, ancient body. The cat was seventeen years old, and deaf. She had not seen it jump from the counter. "You should have warned me," she said.

She lit a cigarette, and waited for the police to come back on the line. She replayed the scene in her mind. There was something about his face . . . a sadness . . . an expression . . . something she could not explain. He seemed like a man lost, with no place to go, no purpose. A loner, someone who does not have a friend in the world.

12:00 p.m. The Nursery

Annie made rounds. The nurses were busy with their duties. One was recording vital signs, another helping a lab tech draw blood samples. Two were showing the firemen how to bag-breathe a tiny infant. Annie stopped to watch. One of the firemen, rugged with brown hair and perfect eyebrows, quickly got the hang of it, and he grinned at Annie.

The hum of activity was overshadowed by the howling of the storm. Conversations rose and fell with the wind. Occasionally, a nurse would run to the cafeteria. This stressed the remaining staff, having to cross-cover the additional patients, but they were used to this, and everyone hated going without meals.

In spite of all the expertise and experience on the unit, Annie knew how quickly things could go wrong. Everyone had to learn, but they carried a heavy load of guilt when mistakes were made. The suffering and the deaths were tragic and draining, and yet there were many rewards—all the babies did not die.

Nostalgia came over Annie. Just a month ago, the NICU had held their first preemie reunion. Four hundred children, and their parents, filled the Shiner's Temple. Annie had gone with mixed feelings, and had been overwhelmed. A number of the children had developed normally, but there were those who suffered the residuals of their premature birth. Some were blind, some could not talk or walk—and never would. A few like Kerry, had managed to survive. These were the ones who played havoc with Annie's heart. None were even close to being normal.

Annie had watched a mother carefully spooning cake and ice cream into her blind child's mouth. She saw an entertainer in a dog costume pause, and then hurry away from this child. The children who could not walk, rode in specially adapted chairs, and were wheeled around by their overprotective mothers. One mother told Annie that even though her daughter could not walk, or eat properly, she excelled in school, and was at the head of her class.

Another child broke Annie's heart, taking root in her memory like a wildflower. She was blind, her legs retracted in a fetal position. Only half the size of a normal child her age, she was being pulled in a brightly painted wagon by her eight-year-old twin brother. The little girl sang a song for Annie, about a train climbing a mountain. These children haunted her soul. Here was her life's work, and she could not put a price on it.

Annie's thoughts returned to the present.

The nursery lights flickered, and multiple conversations were interspersed with monitor alarms that had to be reset.

The emergency generators were now in place. The biggest threat was always the possibility of fire or explosion. An electrical spark could ignite the main oxygen line. Once, Annie had seen a spark shoot up the tubing of a respirator. The nurse caring for the baby reacted with lightning speed. She disconnected the respirator and yelled '*fire*,' while another nurse grabbed an extinguisher and quickly doused the flame. When the danger was past, the two had collapsed in hysterical laughter. The fire safety committee brought this incident up every year at their annual fire in-service. The following day, Annie had brought each of these amazing nurses a plastic fireman hat.

Annie watched the windows, and wondered if they would hold. The high winds worried the firemen. Annie could not remember any previous storms lasting this long.

Someone knocked on the double doors and Jeffrey pushed the automatic opener. A short, crippled man with a brace on one leg stood there grinning. He was holding a large cardboard box with a decorated cake. He also had a plate of deviled eggs. It was their regular volunteer, Cooper Graham.

"Coop," Annie said, amazed. "How did you get though the lobby?"

"I told them I was a parent," he said. "They were too busy to bother with me."

"You should have taken the day off," Annie said, but she was always glad to see him. He had been volunteering for years. He had polio as a child, and had been a patient in this hospital. He volunteered on every holiday, and he always brought a treat.

Annie put the cake on the desk in the nurses station. Jeffrey brought a stack of plastic throw-away cups and some new wooden tongue blades.

"Food," Annie yelled over the intercom.

They took turns leaving their stations momentarily for cake. Stabbing at the cake with the tongue blades made a mess on the floor. A fireman stood there grinning. "I wish my wife could see me eating out of a specimen cup."

Annie craved a cigarette, but ate a deviled egg. She smelled smoke on the intern, Kathleen, and knew she must have taken a break.

She asked Jeffrey to find Magic, and see if the dog would clean up the crumbs.

"He's in the laundry room—away from the windows," Jeffery responded.

Phillips came in, took a small piece of cake and sat down at the desk. After a few bites, he lost interest, and dumped the cake in the trash. His face was still pale, but he was not sweating. He looked at Annie and asked, "Are you going to be on the Ethics Board?"

She was surprised, and flustered, that he would bring up the topic.

"Why would you think that?"

"I think you'd be good." He stopped, and covered his mouth during a coughing spell. He continued, "Someone will have to fight for our babies. You would be their voice."

She sighed. "I'm not really good enough to play God."

"Nobody is good enough to play God."

I know that, she thought, and looked into his eyes and wondered: *Do you play God?* She wanted to ask about Jessie's death, but this was not the time or place.

Phillips got up and the moment was lost. "Let's make some quick rounds." They went to the bedside of the newest admissions, twins born at home during the night.

"*Failed Home Births*" was written in bold letters across Phillips' clipboard; he showed it to Annie. The twins were septic with Group B Strep, an infection passed on from their mother.

"A massive dose of antibiotics, a respirator to breathe until they recover, and some careful monitoring is all they need," Phillips said. The bigger twin, named Jake, was already off the respirator and in a low percent of oxygen. He was sucking on a blue pacifier, and a note taped over his crib read: *Wake me and you will carry me around.*

"He's hungry," said his nurse, a petite redhead with slightly crooked teeth, and an unfamiliar face. She was from the hospital's float pool. Her nametag read '*Sheila.*'

"Well, Sheila, tell him he can't eat for another twenty-four hours, but he will eat." Phillips said, and smiled. Annie saw his old familiar smile.

"What about Jill?" Phillips said, nodding at the sister.

"She's sicker," the nurse said, with a worried frown. "I doubt she will come off her respirator today." She had covered the baby's eyes with a diaper to shade them. She said timidly, "May I ask you something else, Sir?"

"Don't call me sir," Phillips interjected. "I only make the interns do that." He tried to laugh but it came out in a cough.

"What do you think of home deliveries?"

"Home deliveries are for pizzas," he said. Annie had to smile at his familiar remark.

"More and more women are having them," Sheila said. "They want a more relaxed atmosphere. They don't like hospital settings."

He looked at the twins, frowned, and said, "You take a chance with someone else's life. Someone who might want to live for eighty or ninety years is being born under stupid conditions. And this, just so you can feel more at ease. I wouldn't do it."

"Is it okay to give Jill an admission bath? She hasn't had one yet."

"No," Annie said. "We might have to evacuate."

Annie and Phillips left the pod.

"Let's hope we don't have to evacuate," Phillips said, and Annie saw that he was again sweating profusely.

"Are you okay?"

"Damn it! I'm all right." He looked away. "Why do people keep asking me that?" He bumped into a utility cart and leaned against the wall.

Annie did not say anything.

"Molly's on the phone," Jeffrey yelled.

Annie walked with him, and saw his face light up briefly. He then clamped his lips together, and his face took on the hard sullen look she had seen earlier.

He stopped. "Tell her I'm busy," he said. He gripped his shoulder and Annie saw that his knuckles were white.

The bastard's back, she thought, but what are these mixed signals?

Phillips walked away saying nothing more. He continued down the hall, and stopped at Kerry's cubicle. He watched Fancy try to calm the agitated baby. She was pounding on Kerry's chest with a small rubber mask, trying to loosen the mucus that collected in her lungs. Phillips reached out and briefly touched the wall. When Fancy noticed him, he nodded, and went on.

Annie followed him into the nurses station. She began to update the assignment board, aware of his presence behind her. The last time they had spoken, she noticed that his pupils were dilated. The printer, unattended, was spitting out pages of lab work.

A light flashed and Annie answered it. Blake was calling them to the ECMO baby.

Doctor Johnson was listening to the baby's chest. He was using his own stethoscope, a gift from his mother. Earlier, he had shown Annie his name in delicate golden lettering on the ear piece. Annie knew he was becoming more confident. His hands were steady on the baby, and for the first time, Phillips did not crowd him out of the way.

"The baby's acting funny," Blake said. "I wonder if he might have bled into his brain when we changed the machine." Blake was sweating heavily, a line of perspiration across his lips forming a mustache. He was usually calm in a crisis, but the pod was hot, with the air conditioning going off and on. Libby was suctioning the baby and did not comment.

The rain continued to beat against the windows as the wind howled. Phillips was looking at blood gas results. He shook his head. "A fucking air conditioner might help." He squinted as he looked at the readout on the monitor. Blake handed him a washcloth from a basin on the counter. "I'm starting to sweat like the proverbial pig," Phillips muttered.

"And act like one, too," Blake said. He jumped back, with his arms over his face in mock defense.

Phillips surprised them all by laughing at Blake's exaggerated joke. The washcloth helped Phillips' mood. He looked at the clock, and turned to the baby.

Annie watched as he assessed the baby, his hands gentle as they moved across the puffy body. He lightly touched the swollen fontanel on the baby's head. He avoided the IV needle taped above the baby's ear.

She remembered a night several months ago. Phillips was having trouble weaning one of his baby pigs off a respirator. He had stayed with it all evening. He called up to the unit just as she was going off duty, "Annie, can you come and sit with my pig? I can't leave the little fellow unattended, and I have to cross-cover at the university."

He had paid her from his own pocket. She remembered how he had spoken to the pig, down on his knees, and making eye contact. He had been very happy at that time, working on something to help a newborn's lungs.

She wondered now, watching him examine the ECMO baby, what had happened.

What had taken away his joy?

1:30 p.m. The Nursery

Annie went to do Del-baby's care. This was the part of her job that she enjoyed most. After bathing and weighing her, Annie planted a soft kiss on the baby's head. The baby was gaining weight, now that she was finally on full-strength formula. Everything about her was stable today. Her lab values were normal, her blood gases good. Guy had written '*WOW*' over her last results, and had added a happy face.

She changed the linen in the isolette, and cleaned the surfaces with a special solution. When everything was neat and clean, to her nurse's satisfaction, she sat down to write her notes. Annie closed her eyes, feeling a tug in her heart, a memory from years ago. Annie remembered the baby she had lost. Dead in her womb at five months. The size of this tiny girl.

She remembered the drug-induced labor in the delivery room, the doctor's voice: "It was a boy, Annie." He had been taken away while she lay drugged. She had never touched him—never held him—never named him or said goodbye.

Jackson, knowing little of the American way of death, amazingly handled all the details. He traveled the three hundred miles to bury the shoe-box-sized coffin in the grave of Annie's grandfather, a man he had never known. When he returned, they held each other and cried.

She thought about her baby, imagined Jackson standing alone that snowy morning, someone throwing dirt into the tiny grave holding the miniature coffin.

He would be twenty-three. They had made such elaborate plans. *What would he have been like?* Yes, she knew a mother's loss, the pain that never completely goes away. She resolved to ask Jackson about that time. She wanted to be taken there. They would design a stone and have it placed. He had only passed through this world, but deserved a marker.

Annie picked up Del-baby, and sat on the stool near her isolette. She looked at the perfect little face, eyes open, resting quietly in her arms. She listened to the music box she had given her on her first-week birthday.

Doctor Blair came up quietly behind her, softly calling her name. Annie was delighted to see the grin on his face as he watched her holding the baby. Like Annie, he loved the babies.

"Lucky you, Annie. None of my nurses are experiencing such joy today." He leaned back and lounged against the wall. His physical presence was a comfort to her. She now felt at ease with him, knowing she had once made an agonizing choice, but that it would no longer haunt her.

She shook off her melancholy. It seemed like yesterday that he had gone away. He had worn a sliver of a mustache and sideburns, trying to make his youthful face appear older. Now his thick red hair was laced with gray. He had aged well, but he had aged. There were many new lines around his eyes.

"I can remember when your nursery was two small rooms," he said, as he gestured with his arms. "This place is huge, and yet you had the same number of patients way back then." He smiled, and waited for her to speak. She could smell the strong scent of the green-soap they used in the operating room. His hands and arms were pink from scrubbing.

"How does it feel to be back?" She wished she had thought of something more clever or witty to say. He was close enough to touch. She was glad she was holding the baby.

"I feel like it's a different hospital." He gestured with his arms. "I could easily get lost."

"When I saw your name posted in the job search, I wasn't sure you would want to come back," Annie said, flushing—the past hung there between them.

"It's best to let the ghosts out of the closet, don't you think?" He paused. "Are you married, Annie?"

"Yes."

"Any kids?"

"No." She hurried on with the questioning. "Are you married?"

"Was—not now. Married to my work you could say, but lucky enough to have two kids, a boy and a girl. They keep me alive and young."

He paused, started to leave, then turned back. "All these years I only wanted to ask you one question. I still need the answer if you wouldn't mind. Answer it, and I promise I won't mention it again. Why didn't you answer any of my letters or phone calls?"

Her heart beat faster as the years fell away in her mind. Once more, they were standing in the hospital's quaint little courtyard, that still existed. She saw them together snuggling in the secrecy of his hospital call room.

That summer, his wife had left him and gone back to Texas. Annie had known he was married. The whole hospital gossiped about the way his wife treated him. She was always calling him while on duty, demanding that he come home, and threatening to leave. When she finally left, he appeared to be happy.

Annie was unattached and vulnerable. He was a handsome surgeon. They worked together like a team. She had fallen madly in love with him.

Then that day—that Fourth of July—when she came to work, and saw the look of pity on the other nurses' faces, she knew something terrible had happened. She had put her hands over her ears, but they had told her.

His wife had killed herself.

Annie looked now at the pain on his face as he too remembered.

"I want you to know what happened. My wife didn't kill herself because of me, or because of you."

Oh God, he was going to talk about it and she wanted to block it out. The images were coming back . . . the woman sealed in a parked car with the motor running . . . the face, cherry-red from the carbon monoxide.

"She was pregnant," he said.

Annie stood up and put Del-baby back in her isolette. She carefully positioned the baby as he went on with his story.

"It was such a mess, Annie. I was overwhelmed with her problems. It was all in her note. She was carrying twins, and she'd had an amniocentesis. The babies had a genetic defect."

Annie felt like she had been hit with a fist. She bit the inside of her cheek and welcomed the pain. She waited for him to finish.

"She killed herself because of them. They weren't my babies. She left me for someone else. He was the father, not me."

Annie turned and saw the sadness on his face. She reached out and briefly touched his arm.

"I'm so sorry," she said. "The truth is, I was afraid. I was very young, and I wasn't brave enough to follow you. I should have answered your calls. I should have learned the truth."

He nodded. "It's okay Annie, I'm glad to see you again, and know that you are happy. Somehow things worked out for both of us. And we've both been given second chances."

He started to say something, when Blake came running. "I'm so glad to see you, Doctor Blair. Are you coming to see the ECMO baby? I think he's a little better."

Blair turned, and immediately went with Blake. Annie finished her charting, thoughts still whirling in her head. His wife's death had not been their fault. She could let go of the deep guilt. And, at least, there was one consolation: They had both survived, and it was apparent that he was now happy with his life. He had children, and she had gone on to a good life. She would not think of those two children, if they had inherited his red hair, or his skills.

Annie headed back to the ECMO pod. They were all praising Doctor Rustov, and discussing how much he meant to the hospital. "He did a great job changing the pump," Blake said. "That man is an expert. I wish he was staying on. We need him."

"What about the gunshot victim?" the intern asked.

"He's still on life support, but there is no brain activity," Blair said. "We're waiting for his mom to decide about the organ donation."

Doctor Blair shrugged his shoulders, and slowly shook his head.

Annie stood back, feeling numb, as if in a dream. *She was not to blame. His wife had her own demons.*

Blair went on, "We're going to harvest his kidneys in a few hours, if his mother decides that she wants a part of him to live on. I hope she feels that way. Yesterday, we lost a little boy because they couldn't find a liver."

"Life goes on for lucky people, sometimes," Guy said. He winked at Annie.

Blair turned to Annie and smiled. "Indeed it does." And he hurried away.

"I like that man," Guy said. "Did you know him when he was here as a resident?"

"Yes, I knew him," Annie said.

"Was he as good as they say?"

"Even better," she said. She tried to keep her normal voice. "You'll soon find out."

"About my house," Guy said, "the man still says he won't give us a thirty-day extension so we could try to raise the money." He frowned and looked away.

"The bastard," Annie whispered.

"Annie, I've never heard you swear like that." He was called away before she could respond.

Yes, she thought, here I am good old Annie . . . always fair . . . perfect nurse . . . wonderful on the ethics board. But I do not want it, she thought. My life has been too lopsided, always medicine. I need a whole new direction.

She had certainly learned some things today. For a brief moment, she allowed herself to imagine what her life would have been like with Blair. Then Jackson came into her thoughts, his smiling face. I am lucky, she thought, I have a good man who loves me.

Annie turned and saw that Libby was in trouble. She was panting softly, a fine line of perspiration on her forehead. She looked up and said, "I'm having contractions."

"Jesus!" Phillips said, having overheard. "We don't need another preemie. How many weeks are you?" He was 'all doctor' now, with no anger in his voice.

"Thirty-six weeks tomorrow," Libby said. They all looked over at the ECMO baby. It too, was a thirty-six-weeker.

"A month early," Phillips frowned as he calculated. "Your doctor could be off by a couple of weeks. Maybe you are closer to term than he thinks. Why the hell are you in here working?"

Annie put up her hand to stop him. "Some people have to work. Come on, Libby, it's going to be okay."

"Let's get you off your feet," Phillips said "We're not going to let anything happen to your baby."

Annie called for Mac to take Libby into the nursing lounge where there was a couch. Phillips stayed to help Blake with the ECMO baby.

Annie did some shuffling of the staff, and there was no grumbling. "Libby's in labor," she explained. Two nurses agreed to take a double assignment, adding babies to their care who were not in immediate danger.

When Annie got to the lounge, Mac had pulled the old, shabby, chintz-covered couch away from the wall, and had brought in a couple of pillows from the parent room. Annie returned to the nursery, and notified the supervisor. Mac ran in and out, checking on her patients, and delegating duties to others as needed.

Libby had only been lying there a few minutes, when her membranes ruptured.

Annie returned, put her hand on Libby's rock-hard abdomen, and tried to time a contraction. Libby's face blanched with pain, as she arched her back and moaned. When the contraction subsided, Libby turned her face to the wall and wept. "Oh, Annie, I didn't want another baby right now, and I'm afraid I'm going to lose it."

"Libby, you are not going to lose it." Annie took a blue scrub top from a stack of clean laundry, and wiped Libby's face. She then got several towels to put under Libby. "I don't know a pregnant woman who doesn't get depressed at times. Of course you want this baby." She laid her fingers across Libby's wrist to check her pulse. "You're a good mother and you're going to be a good mother with this one."

"I only had three more days to go until my maternity leave. I thought I could handle one more day. I needed the money."

Annie held her, and let her cry. "It's okay, Lib. It's okay."

Jeffrey came in. "Phillips has ordered me to sit with Libby. I'm afraid I feel like that woman in Gone with the Wind. I don't know nothin about birthin no baby." He tried to joke.

"You're the only person we can spare right now," Annie said.

"Doctor Phillips said she must relax. He's trying to get a call through to the medical center. Biggs said the storm has let up a little, but there's another one coming through."

"I've always thought a children's hospital should have its own maternity ward," Annie said. "Right now we have tiny babies being delivered in hospital emergency rooms."

"Phillips said he could deliver you, if he has to," Jeffrey added.

"Tell him to stick to his own advice about relaxing," Libby said, gritting her teeth through another contraction. "Ask him if he's ever had a baby."

Annie timed the contraction. They were hard, but not yet getting any closer.

Jeffrey's smile was sheepish. "Please tell that kid to stay put."

Libby laid her hands on her belly. "Stay put," she demanded. "Do you hear what Jeffrey said? Stay put."

They could hear the wind picking up again. "At least we don't have a window in here that can blow," Jeffrey said.

Tess had gone to help with the ECMO baby. Guy was helping Blake, until Tess could hand over her assignment to a nervous supervisor, who had been called to assist them. "Go on," Annie said to Tess. "I'll give her your report."

Alma was middle-aged, and pear-shaped. She had been a nursing supervisor for many years, but now only worked part-time. "I've only handled big kids most of my life," she told Annie. "I've always been afraid of these little ones."

Annie sensed the woman's fear. "I'm sorry you have to jump into this mess, but we are grateful to have your help." Annie quickly went over the care plan. Alma could not take her eyes off the infant in front of her. He was moving his head slightly.

"You can't leave him alone when he's awake. If that tube comes out of his throat, please call for help, immediately. It's already been replaced once today and his throat is swollen. We might have trouble getting it back in."

"How long have you been doing this kind of nursing?" Alma asked. Annie knew what Alma was really asking. *Do you think I can do this?*

Alma had thick black hair, pulled back with a headband. It seemed to make her head look very large. "It's a wig," Alma said. "I know it looks strange, but I had a bout with cancer and the chemo caused me to lose my hair. It grew back very patchy."

"I'm sorry," Annie said. "I know I was staring."

"I'm used to it. Tell me, how can you work with these babies? They seem so sad. Do they all die?"

"No. No, they don't all die."

Alma turned to talk to the baby. "No, Alex." She laughed, and grabbed a tiny mittened hand. "You can't play with that tube, big guy." She leaned over the crib and tapped his nose. His eyes brightened with her touch. He kicked his feet and tried to reach her glasses. Alma gave him his pacifier, and he calmed down and began to suck.

There was a burst of laughter from the back of the nursery. "Sometimes we even laugh here. It helps to keep us from crying."

Annie noticed that the light in Kerry's room had come on and off while she was talking. "The baby in that cubicle is critical. She could die any time. If you hear that nurse call for help, go over if you can, but don't leave Alex unless he's quiet."

The crib next to Alex was draped with a sheet. "This baby will be easier to care for. He's comatose. His delivery was complicated, and he went without oxygen for too long. His body is perfect, he's beautiful, but he doesn't respond to touch. When you have time, pick him up and hold him, but know this—he will break your heart." Alma's face had a look of terror. I am giving her too much, Annie thought, and tried to relax as she talked. "His mother comes in every day, bathes him, dresses him, and holds him briefly. None of us can watch her."

Guy yelled for Annie, and she had to leave Alma alone with Alex. She paused at the doorway and watched as Alma began talking to Alex in her high-pitched voice. Alex looked at her with his E.T. face not smiling. Alma climbed onto the padded stool, and took his mittened hands. She began to sing. Alex stopped crying and listened.

Alma turned to see Annie watching.

"I can do this," Alma said. "I'm a good nurse and I can do this."

Alma had a big gold watch pinned to her gown. When she let go of Alex's hand, he tried to reach for the watch. Alma removed the mittens and leaned over the crib. Alex's busy fingers closed on the smooth shiny surface of the watch. His eyes widened with surprise.

"We can do this together, Alex," Alma said.

Annie hurried away to the ECMO pod.

1:30 p.m. On the Street

Jessie's father left the area of the store he had robbed, and drove back to his old neighborhood. He parked in his normal place. He saw the curtain flapping in his apartment's open window, the wind driving the rain into the room. He laughed, thinking the landlady would have a mess to clean up. Mary never liked the place anyway. My dog, he thought, why did she take my dog?

Rain sleeted against the windshield, and bits of hail drummed down on the hood. He gulped two beers and ate half of a sandwich. Nothing relieved the ache in his gut. The wind rocked the car, but he was not afraid. There were few vehicles traveling on the street. A police car crawled past, followed by an ambulance. It was time to get out of there.

He turned the key and was surprised when the old engine instantly took hold. He was lucky with the car today. He was too far from the hospital to walk in this storm.

The road blurred in front of him as the windows steamed over. The defrosters did not work, and he swiped at the glass with a dirty rag he kept on the dashboard. The wipers squeaked like new chalk balking on a blackboard. He tried to concentrate—make a good plan—but the beer made him sleepy, and distorted his thoughts. He turned on the radio but heard only static. The lightning strikes were now going all the way to the ground.

At the blinking stoplight, he knew he was close to the park. The window on the driver's side would not completely close, and the rain splashed onto his face and glasses. He counted blocks for it was now impossible to read the street signs.

The steering wheel was wet and slippery in his hands. He hit a pothole and the car lurched. He slammed on the brakes and the car spun on its bald tires and came to rest against the side of a parked pickup. His head thumped the steering wheel and he cried out in pain.

"Ah . . . shit . . ." He rested against the back of the seat and sucked on his bruised fingers. The bandage had come off the burn, but the swelling was gone, and he could bend it. *His trigger finger worked perfectly.*

A thunder clap was followed by a cracking sound, and a large tree fell across the hood. The car shook as if it, too, was in pain.

What was he doing here? Where was Mary? Then the doctor's face came to mind: The man with the funny colored skin, and blue eyes that always looked at him with hate.

"Bastard," he said. "I'm coming." He would have to cut through the park. The storm would not stop him, nothing would. He rubbed his forehead. He needed to talk to Mary. She would help him.

His head cleared. He would find a place to hide in the hospital and work out his plan. He pulled a garbage bag from the clutter on the back seat. Inside he placed two beers, a sandwich, his cigarettes, and the chips. His thirst was powerful, but he had no time to drink now.

He sorted through layers of junk and found the scrub suit he had stolen from the parent room the night a nurse had let him sleep there.

He patted his thigh and felt the hard form of the gun. He took it out, wrapped it in plastic from the sandwich, and pushed the gun back into his pocket.

He found an empty pizza box under the front seat. This would be his ticket into the hospital. Someone was always delivering pizza. The guards usually waved them on.

It was difficult getting out of the car. The wind was in control. He tried to fasten the plastic raincoat, but he gave up—he was already wet. He could feel bits of hail hitting his face. He put his glasses in his pocket.

Walking against the wind, he staggered, holding tight to his bag. There was the sound of a siren in the distance. He was in the park. He focused on the doctor. His rage gave him the strength to fight the wind.

The roar in his ears was deafening. He made it past the swings as the seats crashed like cymbals in a band. The wind knocked him to the ground. He crawled forward, dragging the bag. He could see the outline of the play tunnel made of giant concrete pipes. He got to his knees, but the wind knocked him back, roaring like a locomotive. He made it to the tunnel.

He crawled inside pulling his bag. He put his hands to his face and felt them trembling. His eyes burned. He drew his body into a ball, and put the garbage bag under his head.

He was again alone in the world. Most of his life he had spent alone. Mary was gone, and her name echoed in his head. Like a child, he cried for his mother. A tortured memory emerged: A night when he was five.

It was winter. His mother was ill, laid off from her job as a housekeeper. They lived in one room to conserve heat. His mother never told him about his father. He had no father.

The painted lady that lived next door, the one with the fat, nylon covered legs and chunky shoes, had brought them a loaf of bread. It was still warm, and he had immediately eaten his share. His mother then cooked an apple, and covered it with their last bit of margarine. She gave him half. It was not enough to stop his hunger.

They had a skinny yellow dog that begged for crumbs. His mother, her thin face hidden under a thick woolen scarf, had given the dog a piece of the apple and given the rest to him. His mother had coughed far into the night. In the morning, the painted lady came, and told him to come home with her. "Where's my mother?" "She's gone, child." The lady helped him dress, her crippled hands fumbling with his shoes.

It was only after the funeral, when the Catholic sister, her plump face framed in starched white cotton, came to take him to the orphanage, that he understood what '*gone*' meant.

Everyone he had ever loved was gone—his mother—Mary—his baby—his dog.

1:45 p.m. The Subbasement

Bubby awakened inside the isolette. He turned on his side, and kicked at the door. It opened slightly, but was facing the wall. He was unable to squeeze through the opening. He called several times for his mother. He found his bottle, sucked eagerly on the nipple, and drifted back to sleep.

1:45 p.m. The Emergency Room

Bobby-J sat on the gurney, holding her swollen jaw. She was agitated, and had been coaxed into allowing a doctor to give her a shot.

"Bubby," she called out, "have they found my Bubby?"

A nurse, a redhead with a colorful bow tied around the end of her stethoscope, came to her aid. "No," she said, "but we have his picture now. Your mother brought it in. She has your other children."

The nurse began to fill a container with suckers, and she kept talking to Bobby-J as she worked. "The police are going to walk through the neighborhood and show his picture, as soon as the storm lets up."

Bobby-J stood, shaking uncontrollably, and immediately collapsed, weeping, into the nurse's arms. "I'm a good mother," she said.

The pathetic teenage voice reached the nurse's heart—she often held sobbing mothers. The job had somewhat hardened her heart, but she, too, had a small son. Her eyes filled with tears, as she held tightly to Bobby-J, the mother's sobs shaking both bodies.

1:45 p.m. The Lobby

The lobby was crowded with people taking refuge from the storm. Biggs stood at the reception desk and counted the children and adults. He listened to fragmented conversations as he walked around.

A large picture of Bubby was posted on the wall by the elevator. The city police had made copies and were going to go through the neighborhood.

Biggs saw the elderly man who came in daily, Jolly Rogers. The staff knew him, and he never bothered the children. Biggs went over.

Jolly was taking soda pop cans from the trash, transferring them to a worn plastic bag reading: *Jesus Saves.*

"Jolly, we've got a little boy missing. Look at this picture. Have you seen him?"

Jolly held the picture close to his watery eyes. He looked up, frowned, and looked at the picture again. He nodded his head, and pointed. "He went over there." He pointed to the wall. "There," Jolly repeated, and turned back to his task.

Biggs looked towards the wall. There was only the picture of Bubby. He must mean that picture, Biggs thought.

He walked to the wall and stared. A dimpled face, with baby teeth, grinned back.

Bubby, a little boy not quite two years old—holding a truck.

Where are you Bubby?

1:45 p.m. The Nursery

In the nursery, everyone's nerves were on edge. Libby was resting in the lounge, her labor had slowed down. At least for now, she was not having the hard contractions. Phillips came in with an ultrasound machine. They watched the outline of the infant. He got a close-up of a tiny hand, and they saw the sex organ of the male. "Another boy," Libby said. "I can't believe it's another boy." She laughed, overcome with the peek at her son.

"I see a perfect baby," Phillips said. He stopped the ultrasound when a contraction started. Annie adjusted the rate of an IV Phillips had ordered after being in touch with Libby's obstetrician.

Magic paced nervously in the hall. They worked around him.

The phones continued to ring. The pneumatic tube system had been shut down after someone found liquid from a broken container. The lab specimens now had to be hand carried, causing a delay in all blood gas results.

"Just like the good ol' days," Mackenzie said to Annie, as she handed a specimen to Jeffrey.

Phillips was standing at the desk. "People talk about the good old days. Believe me, there were no good old days except for the man who had money." He put his head down and appeared to mumble.

A fireman brought Phillips a copy of blood gas results from the ECMO baby, who was slowly showing improvement.

Kerry, Valium-dosed again, was in a drugged sleep. Fancy sat at her bedside, biting her nails.

Phillips got up and began to pace in the hallway.

The intern, Kathleen, whispered to Annie that she was going to the 'little girl's room.'

Doctor Johnson was standing in pod one joking with a student nurse. "I'm getting the hang of some things," he said. "At least I know all my patients' names."

The night-chief had come on early to help them, but had been immediately called away to a Code Blue in the ICU.

• • •

The lightning was awesome. The full fury of the storm was on them. As Annie went into pod one, Magic stopped in the hall, remained motionless, then howled.

The window in pod one exploded. Glass, debris, and rain blew into the nursery. The monitors alarmed, and the lights flickered, as the power failed. Almost immediately, the firemen activated the emergency generators.

• • •

They could hear the steady sound of the rain through the open window. The worst appeared to be over. The firemen quickly rigged a tarp over the opening.

The two babies from pod one were safe, having been moved closer to the doorway, and their cribs covered with sheets. Annie was covered with dirt, but unharmed.

Guy came running to check the equipment. "Listen," he said, "the wind has stopped."

Doctor Johnson had blood pouring from a gash in his scalp. Mac immediately went to his aid, pressing a wad of cotton over his wound.

Phillips went from pod to pod checking on patients, as the nurses and doctors quickly reset monitors.

"Everyone is fine," Phillips called to Annie.

Jeffrey came in from the lounge. "Libby's fine, but the phone in there is dead."

"What a holiday," Mac said.

"Holiday pay, remember," someone added.

"Yeah, but not until the new contract comes out at Christmas," another voice chimed in.

"We need hazard pay, like the military," Jeffrey said. He tripped over an electrical line and grabbed at Annie. She fell backwards into Phillips, whose arms closed around her. Annie was shocked as she felt his bony chest. He helped her stand and backed away.

The rain was gentle now and the storm seemed to be over. Annie wondered where Jackson was, and if he was thinking of her.

Annie turned to Jeffrey. "See if you can find a housekeeper to clean up this mess."

Mackenzie came out of Kerry's room. "Would you believe, she slept through the whole thing?" Annie nodded and took a deep breath, she still had work to do.

A young, gangly fireman came into the nurses station. "All the patients are on emergency power, but they hope to have your power restored in about an hour. We'll be moving our equipment out at that time." As he started to leave, he turned, and gave Annie a quick thumbs-up.

"You fellows have been wonderful," Annie said.

"Any time."

"Maybe we could have some lunch now," Guy said. The rain had nearly stopped, and the sky had lightened considerably.

Annie went into pod one. "Don't move these babies until they get that window fixed. I'm going to check on Libby. Perhaps we can move her now."

"She's tough," Jeffrey said. "That lady is really something. I like her."

"She likes you, too," Annie said. "We all do." He grinned, blushed, and went back to the computer.

• • •

A housekeeper on the second floor had watched the storm in action. She told Biggs that she had seen a funnel cloud take out the houses along the edge of the park. "Blowing them to pieces. Just like the wolf in the Three Little Pigs." Then the twister had veered into the side of the parking garage taking out a wall. "It sent those cars spinning down onto the freeway like tops."

Biggs had glimpsed the devastation in the park. All the recently donated trees, painstakingly planted by the Boy Scouts, were gone. The little dogwoods lay lifeless, scattered like discarded drinking straws.

2:10 p.m. The Park

In the tunnel, Jessie's father was protected. Even though the storm appeared to be over, he waited in the wet, stuffy confines of his shelter. He was not a man that valued clean, fresh outside air. His wheezy raspy breathing was the only sound in his ears. Then he heard something. It was the soft chirping of a cricket that must have taken refuge from the storm. He felt the urge to find and smash it, but remembered that Mary liked crickets. He crawled out of the shelter pulling his bag.

The sun was shining and it burned his face. He tore off the plastic raincoat and threw it aside.

There was destruction everywhere. Leaves and broken branches littered the play area. The swings were uprooted, the poles lying twisted on the ground.

He fumbled for a cigarette and watched a fire truck back up to the hospital entrance. He squinted and put on his glasses to get a better look. Firemen were loading equipment, and a group of uniformed men, assisted by young boys, were clearing debris from the driveway.

He reached into his bag, got a can of beer, and guzzled it down. He had plenty of time. He would wait in the park until the fire truck left. He knew that Phillips was on duty today. He had seen the call list the night Jessie was dying. He closed his eyes, and he could see that schedule.

His clothes had started to dry. His thoughts turned to Mary. He thought he heard her calling. He saw a woman pushing a stroller along the walk next to the park. She had long blonde hair.

It was not his Mary.

2:30 p.m. The Nursery

Annie thanked the firemen who had helped with the cleanup. All the damage was confined to the first pod. Biggs told the staff that a window had also blown on another floor. No children had been injured. He mentioned that a nurse was injured when she slipped on a wet floor. "And for once, it wasn't housekeeping's fault," he said.

Doctor Johnson had the unit's only injury. It had taken twenty stitches to close the wound. He was examined in the emergency room, but returned to the unit, after the x-rays of his skull appeared normal. Phillips had excused him for the rest of the shift, but he chose to stay on duty. "I'm just getting the feel of the place. I know my patients now, and I love seeing them improve."

"We're happy to have you back," Annie said. She saw his face brighten with the remark.

The emergency squad was on the way for Libby.

Annie had changed into clean scrubs, but she still felt grimy. There had been no time for a shower. The staff was behind in patient care, and everyone worked at a quickened pace. There was no conversation.

The nursery remained hot. The air conditioner had come on briefly, and then gone off. It had been a reoccurring problem all summer.

Phillips now complained of feeling cold, while everyone else sweltered. He was wearing a long-sleeved top under his scrubs. He was withdrawn and sullen again, and Annie warned the staff not to approach him with trivial matters.

"Give the interns a chance," she said, in a loud voice. She was sure Phillips had heard, and he had not objected.

A man from maintenance was working on the telephones.

Annie walked to the covered window and Mac joined her. They lifted the tarp and looked at the destruction in the park. The landscaped gardens were gone. Bright red geraniums lay over the street like scarlet ribbons. They could see an old man sitting on the steps of house with a portion of the roof missing. He was patting the head of a large dog.

"Squad's here for Libby," Jeffrey yelled. Annie and Mac went to say goodbye.

Phillips helped put Libby on the cart. "Watch the IV," he said. Libby's face was pale and apprehensive. She looked like a child who had just been told there is no Santa Claus.

Phillips took her hand. "Hey, kiddo," he said, "you're going to get a break from this joint."

Libby tried to smile. "If the baby has any problems, I want it to come here."

"You're going to have a healthy baby. I just know it."

Libby put on a brave smile.

They propped open the nursery doors, and stood silently, as the squad tucked the straps in around Libby.

As they watched, holding their breath, Libby disappeared down the hallway.

At the desk, Fancy was talking with a couple of nurses. They were laughing.

"My car," Fancy said to Annie, "and yours, and three others—" She burst into giggles. "They were blown from the garage and are down on the freeway."

"They're all wrecked," Jeffrey said.

"Oh my God!" Annie said. "Are you sure?"

"Security called us."

Annie couldn't help laughing. "I just had the oil changed and the tires rotated." That really struck them as hilarious.

"You should have driven a junker like I do," Jeffrey said.

"Jackson will never believe it." Annie shook her head in wonder. "Nobody in their right mind would have thought we would lose any cars today."

"Well, I've never liked the color of mine anyway," Fancy said. "George picked it out, and I would have preferred a red one."

Phillips listened to their chatter. "Better a car dead than a baby dead," he said in his poker-faced humor.

"Anything new on the missing kid?" Mac asked.

"Nothing. But I have some good news." Jeffrey beamed.

"Well?"

"The kitchen sent a message that the freezers were damaged by a power surge, and they are giving away all the ice cream before it melts."

"Ice cream gives me a bellyache," Mackenzie said. She was busy wiping down a wall in the first pod.

"Jeffrey, take one of the carts down and get as much ice cream as you can. It won't go to waste up here."

What Annie really wanted was a cigarette, but that was out of the question.

Annie put on a pair of sterile gloves, and went to help Mackenzie fill heparin syringes. The previous batch had been knocked off the counter and was contaminated.

"Let's only do a few, since this fluid bag expires."

They worked quietly, listening to the young nurses talking in the next pod. They were always talking about the funniest things, and it made Annie feel younger. Right now they were discussing whether a man looked sexier in jockey shorts or boxer shorts.

"How about no shorts," Annie interjected.

"Telephone for Mac," Jeffrey called.

Mac picked up the wall phone in pod one, as Annie continued with the syringes. Her mind drifted back to Mark Blair. There were still some unanswered questions from that summer, but she was happy that they had met today. She wanted to know more about his present life. She dared not think about what she would have done, if she had known the truth back then. These thoughts did no good, and she pushed them from her mind.

Annie turned to Mac as she hung up the phone.

Mackenzie was quiet and Annie said, "We've been through a lot together. Now we share this crazy storm."

Mac nodded, but said nothing.

"You're a great gal to work with," Annie said. She wanted to blurt out her plans. She knew Mac would feel cheated, hearing it from the nursing manager, but she was not up to tearful goodbyes today. She loved Mac. Mac was the 'eternal optimist,' like a bird that sings when the weather is gloomy.

Annie was struck with sudden remorse—something sacred was slipping away—she would be searching for new dreams. She paused and watched Mac's deft fingers twirl the syringes into a perfect row, ready to be filled. Mac was ten years younger than Annie. "Don't ever lose your passion for nursing," Annie said, and she gave her a fierce hug.

Mac looked up, and Annie saw that her face was red, and her cheeks were wet.

"Mac! What's the matter?"

Mac continued crying. "I'm such a simpleton. I just talked to mom. Nixon bit the neighbor kid, and he had to go to the emergency room and have his hand sutured."

"Oh, Mac, he didn't. Was the kid teasing Nixon?"

"There's more." Mac took a tissue from Annie and wiped her nose. "It's the second time this week. The seizure drug has completely changed his disposition. The vet said he couldn't be trusted. He told my mom I need to think about having Nixon put to sleep."

"Oh, no! He's like your child." Annie pictured the beautiful Cocker Spaniel with his floppy ears and honey-colored eyes. Mac always kept the dog beautifully groomed. In the car, he rode in a special harness. He even went shopping with her, in a stroller.

Mackenzie straightened up. Her voice was stronger. "My only option would be to keep him locked up at home. Never take him anywhere." She looked at Annie. "He would hate that. I couldn't do that to him."

"Can someone give me a hand?" Fancy yelled, from Kerry's cubicle.

"Please don't mention this to anyone," Mac said. "I don't want to talk about it right now."

Annie nodded, as they hurried to Kerry's crisis.

2:30 p.m. The Lobby

Jessie's father walked from the park with his garbage bag tucked under his arm. He fell in behind a group of Girl Scouts and followed them through the revolving door of the hospital's main entrance. He was sweating, his nerves on edge. He immediately took a seat in the waiting room and slowly looked around.

There was unusual gaiety in the lobby, with a party going on. Young children sat in a circle by the fish tank. Three clowns were doing magic tricks. He watched the clowns with fascination. He remembered the yearly trips to the circus, as an orphan. The children roared with laughter, when one of the clowns bumped into a guard who was setting up folding chairs.

He willed his heart to calm down, and looked at his watch. He reset it to the time on the clock above the admission desk. Several patients came off the elevator, followed by two nurses pushing IV poles. Two of the children were bald and wore masks.

A male nurse, carrying a shopping bag with the hospital's logo, got off the elevator. He set the bag down by a chair across from the admitting desk, and went to help the security guard with the folding chairs.

Jessie's father crossed the lobby, and sat in the chair by the bag. He started when a door opened. A woman, glasses perched on her nose, asked, "May I help you?"

"No . . . no," he mumbled. "I'm waiting for my wife." She stared for a moment, then returned to the office, shutting the door. He could hear a telephone ringing.

He carefully took the pizza box from his bag, and waited. There was a line at the visitor's desk where a volunteer was handing out name tags. He needed one of those tags.

He did not recognize the volunteer, an older man with a bald head. The man's face was lined with fatigue. He was explaining something to a man in a jogging suit. The jogger swung his arm around and struck the lady behind him. She began to loudly complain. In the confusion, Jessie's father rushed forward and said, "Pizza for the NICU." He had no idea of the exact procedure, and worried that they might send someone down.

The man behind the desk was a regular volunteer, extremely proper concerning regulations, but he usually worked as a messenger. He had never worked at the visitor's desk. He motioned Jessie's father toward the elevators without looking up, and without giving him a visitor's badge.

Jessie's father spotted the note posted on the elevator, and quickly pushed the button. He rode to the subbasement, got off, and looked around. The place appeared deserted, although in the distance, he could hear the faint clink of dishes, and the low murmur of voices.

An adjacent elevator suddenly opened, and a housekeeper, pushing an empty crib, got off.

"Help you?" the man said.

"Naw," Jessie's father answered. "I'm waiting for my wife."

The housekeeper continued down the hall. He opened a door, shoved the crib into the room, slammed the door, and returned. He was whistling, and nodded as he got on the elevator.

Jessie's father headed for the door that the housekeeper had just closed. He needed a place to hide. He went in, turned on the light, and closed the door. The door only locked with a key. He cursed.

There were tables and chairs along one wall. He found a folding chair, and wedged it against the door. He saw a cart filled with worn linen and scrubs marked '*use for rags.*' There were several long white coats like the doctors wore. He smiled at his luck when he found one that was not wrinkled. He tried it on. It would do.

There were isolettes and warming beds at the end of the room. The warming bed was like the one his son had died on.

Jessie. Jessie. His thoughts whirled. *Why did you die?*

He spotted a cart filled with toys. A note clipped to the cart read: *Damaged Property of Occupational Therapy.* He noticed a bright yellow pail, with a broken handle. He unzipped his dirty jeans, and peed into the pail.

He sat down and tried to sort out his jumbled thoughts. The room was stuffy, but not unbearable. *What was he doing here?*

His mind was blank. Then he heard a voice, "*The doctor knows. The doctor killed Jessie.*" His anger returned as he thought of the doctor.

He heard a noise—like the sound of a kitten. No, it was the muffled cry of a child. *Where? Jessie?*

He stood, and followed the sound, walking the length of the room. When he reached the isolettes along the wall, he could clearly hear a voice.

"Mommy? Mommy?"

He pulled an isolette away from the wall. The bottom door opened, and a toddler tumbled out. The small blond boy was crying. He was holding an empty baby bottle, and his diaper was leaking.

Bubby stopped crying when he saw the man. He was not afraid. He was used to strangers. His mother sometimes brought new boyfriends home.

It was the kid in the picture posted in the lobby.

"How'd you get in there, kid?"

"Don't know. Where's my mommy?"

"What's your name?"

"Bubby." The boy rubbed his eyes, as they grew accustomed to the light.

He stared at the boy in astonishment. He was healthy, with lots of bright blond hair.

"You got crackers?" Bubby asked.

"All I got is some chips," the man said.

He brought the crumpled bag of chips, and handed it to the boy. He then went to search through the worn linen for something to put on the boy. He found a pair of rather large children's pajamas. He managed to get the diaper off, and dried the boy with a piece of sheet. After he got the pajamas on, Bubby wandered over to the cart with broken toys. He took out a few, put them on the floor, and began to play.

Bubby looked up once, and said, "Mommy?"

"She'll come soon, kid, don't worry."

Jessie's father filled the baby bottle with water, and set it on the floor where Bubby played. He sat down on his chair, and tipped it back against the wall. He closed his eyes and tried to think. He had to get to the NICU.

He had already forgotten about Bubby.

3:30 p.m. The Nursery

The telephone service had been restored. The phones rang constantly as parents called to check on their infants. Worried staff members' families also called.

Jeffrey was overwhelmed, carrying messages from pod to pod as fast as his tired legs could carry him. "I need roller skates," he said to Annie.

The shift had changed at three o'clock for some of the nurses, but no one had yet actually left, as everyone was behind in their charting. Annie was working the report when Jeffrey came running in and said, "There's a hell of a row going on in pod four. Phillips is raging at one of the private doctors."

"Oh no," Annie said. "I don't have time for this."

It was one of Mackenzie's patients. Mac stood at the bedside, her lips in a grim line, her face bright red with anger. She did not acknowledge Annie.

"Don't be a damn fool," Phillips said in an angry voice. "You open this kid up and he'll die immediately. His gut is dead. It's dead, I'm telling you."

The private neonatologist had his own nursery on the other side of the city. He sent his babies to the Children's Hospital only when they were dying. He was a well-dressed man in his forties, his hair cut short, in the student style that was becoming popular. Annie thought it made him look silly. She had not seen him actually touch a patient in years, although he always came in wearing his faithful stethoscope around his neck. He usually looked at the patient, asked the nurse a couple of questions, and then wrote a long note in the patient's history. This assured him of payment for each visit.

When the infant's family had a lot of money—like this one—he chose to handle the case himself. He was a smooth-talker, and could always convince the parents that his decision was the correct one. Annie hated it when he transferred a patient to her unit.

This baby was a tragic case. A nurse or an intern—it was never clear which—had changed a nasal-gastric tube, putting it into the stomach, when the two-pound infant was three days old. The tube had ruptured the stomach, but the fact was not discovered for several hours, until milk feedings were started. The baby's gut died.

The baby had been transferred to them for surgery, but all of his gut was gangrenous. Rustov had opened the belly, looked at the blackened mess, and sutured the belly shut. The baby was sent back to the nursery to die. Here the baby hung now, suspended in limbo for the past week. It was only the excellent nursing care that had kept him alive.

Annie looked at the baby. He was on a morphine drip, because the nurses had rebelled and refused to care for him without the pain medicine. His sparrow chest moved only with the respirator. His eyes were closed. His skin was yellow and dried, but the skin over his distended belly was blue and shiny.

"There are parents in the other pods," Annie said. "We can't have all this yelling."

She did not look at the private doctor. She looked at Phillips and waited for him to tell her what was going on.

Phillips began to pace. His lips were clamped, and his hands were clinched so tightly, they were bloodless. He had a ghostly look, and Annie knew he was going to erupt. He grabbed the edge of the warming bed and turned to Annie. He lowered his voice and said, "Do you know what this bastard wants to do?"

Annie felt her abdomen tighten.

"He wants to open this kid's belly again. He says he read about a couple of documented cases where the gut had rejuvenated. He's actually called in the 'Old Man' for a consult."

"No," Mackenzie swore behind Annie's back. "If the Old Man comes, you'll have to get someone else to take care of this baby. I will not help him." She stared at Annie, her face puffy, ready to explode. They all knew the Old Man. He was seventy years old now, and had botched so many cases, but charges had never been filed against him.

"Don't you remember Noah?" Mac said.

Phillips motioned for the two nurses to follow him to the hallway.

Mac explained. "The Old Man operated on Noah, did the surgery right here on the unit."

"I remember," Annie said. Phillips was trying to recall the patient.

Mac went on. "He didn't want the baby to die in surgery, because it was bad for his statistics."

"I think I was at University Hospital during that time," Phillips said.

"That's not the part that's the problem," Mac said. "It was before we were allowed to give the tiny babies anything for pain. He paralyzed that baby with a drug, so he wouldn't move, and then he operated."

"Mac was forced to assist him. They would have fired her on the spot if she'd refused," Annie said.

Mac wiped her eyes. "I told him that it was criminal to operate on a baby without giving something for pain." She stopped talking as she remembered.

Annie finished her story. "He fired back at her saying that he thought it was criminal for a nurse to talk back to a doctor."

"And I was written up, and reprimanded, for that remark," Mac said.

"Lucky for Noah, he died very quickly after that operation."

Phillips appeared determined now. "Don't worry, Mac. The gut is dead. Tell him this, Annie, for me. I don't want to look at his ugly face again. He will operate on that baby over my dead body." He stalked away.

Annie went back to the pod. The doctor was still standing in the same place, his arms now folded across his chest. She saw the gold watch, the beautifully tailored suit, the silk tie. He gave her a weak smile.

"I haven't seen you in a long time, Annie. Good to see you are still here. You were always my favorite nurse."

There had been a time, long ago, when she liked him, and respected him. He had appeared to be as consumed with medicine as she was. They had spent long hours at the bedsides of critical babies—the best way to get experience. At the time he had excellent skills. Then he had married a rich woman. After that, his decay began. Annie looked at him and believed that he no longer had the right to make decisions about a sick baby.

"This baby is dying," she said. "Surgery won't help him. You need to tell his mother the truth, so she can tell him goodbye."

The doctor drew back in surprise. "Well," he said, in a gruff voice. "I can see who you are siding with now." He tried to retain some dignity. "Maybe this can wait until tomorrow. Is his mother here?"

"She never leaves the hospital. She'll be in the lobby or the cafeteria."

He smiled a sickly smile. "I'll talk to her. She'll listen to me. She'll wait if I ask her too." He straightened up, pulled at the crease in his trousers revealing the expensive Italian shoes, turned, and left.

Phillips returned to the pod, his face marked with fatigue. He went to the baby. "It's okay, little fellow. I've got your back, now. Ain't nobody gonna touch your belly again. I can promise you that." He wrote for an increased dose of morphine.

Mac came in and read the new order. She nodded to Phillips. Annie helped her turn the baby's stiffened body, and prop him in a more comfortable position. "He's starting to get pressure sores," she said. "He's so stiff, it's like turning a block of wood. I can't find the baby in there."

The baby's mother rushed in. She was gray-haired and stooped, her face swollen from crying. She looked like she could be the grandmother. She was forty-five, and this was her first child. Annie and Mac knew that she would stand watch at his bedside—until the end.

Annie returned to the nurses station. Phillips was seated in the corner. He appeared to be agitated, and was tapping his gold pen on the desk. Annie began writing furiously on the nursing report, updating the patients' conditions. She had her back to Phillips.

"If we had an ethics board right now, I would call them," Phillips said.

"About that baby in the back?" Annie swung around to face him.

"You're damn right."

She put down her pen. "What do you think an ethics board might do?"

"They'd want to stop all unnecessary treatment."

Annie sighed. "But who defines unnecessary treatment?"

"I've been wrong about that a lot of times in my life. I remember when we all tried to make ourselves believe that these tiny beings didn't feel pain."

"I've always believed they suffered. I hate every needle stick that draws their blood," Annie said.

"Are you going to, at least, give some thought to this ethics board thing?"

"I don't want to play God."

"We all play God, every minute here," he said. "We hear a heartbeat drop on a monitor, and we intervene. The lab report shows an increased white blood count, and we zap them with an antibiotic. A hemoglobin drops, and we push blood."

"You're right," she said. "I've just never thought about it like that."

Doctor Johnson came into the nurses station and handed a blood gas sheet to Phillips. Phillips read the report, looked up, and said, "What change would you make?"

Doctor Johnson flushed with surprise. "Why . . . I think I'd go up on the pressure by two, Sir."

Phillips studied the sheet again. "I think I would have gone back up on the oxygen, but your idea just might be better. Let's try it. I'm impressed." He handed the sheet back to Johnson, who excitedly hurried away.

Annie looked at Phillips and smiled.

"What? What are you smiling for?"

"You," she said. "You've always been such a good teacher when you wanted to be. There's a famous poet named Robert Bly who said, 'All men are sweet when they are teaching.'"

"Well, I think he's going to make a good doctor."

"I agree. I hope you tell him that."

"I still think you should be on the ethics board."

"I don't know why I was recommended. I got a letter saying I had been nominated by several people. Do people think I'm really the . . . all-wise . . . all-saint?"

"No. They probably think the way I do, that you'd be fair. You would treat each case as special, just like you treat your patients." As Annie went on writing, he said, "I knew you before you became a saint."

"I was the wild one . . . but it's been so long since I've done anything crazy. I'm an old married woman now, you know." She saw the sad thin face before her. She wanted to comfort him, somehow. "You were there in my wilder days, remember?"

Jeffrey came back into the station and announced that he was helping out with the ECMO baby. "I'll answer the phones back there. Just let them ring."

When he left, Annie turned back to Phillips. She was going to ask about Jessie. If he got angry, she would back off. Maybe he would explain why he had been so angry, and had come late to the code.

She said, "I want to ask you about something—"

"I bet I know what it's about. I've always figured you'd get around to asking. That New Year's party, umpteen years ago, before either of us were married, right?"

My God, he was going to bring up that silly night years ago.

It had been the only time in Annie's life, she had been completely drunk.

"You want to know what happened that night, right?"

"Okay." She blushed, and remembered. "I woke up in your bed, naked."

"Nothing happened. You just passed out."

"I woke up terribly hung over, and all my clothes were folded neatly on a chair. You were gone. Yet, I'm supposed to believe that nothing happened."

He smiled. "I had just gotten over the stomach flu, and I didn't drink that night. I had planned to drive you to your apartment, but you threw up all over everything. God, what a mess. I couldn't get an address out of you, and the only things in your purse were a set of keys and a comb." He shook his head.

"I took you to my place, and put you in the shower, then to bed. I washed your clothes and put them on the chair. You slept through everything. You were perfectly safe with me. After all, I am a doctor, I've seen a lot of naked bodies. I had to be on duty at five. That's why I left you."

She saw that he was being truthful. "No wonder my dress was so tight. It wasn't washable. I couldn't understand what happened to it. I never wore it again—and I never got drunk again."

"Since nothing happened, it never crossed my mind that you would have thought differently."

"Well, one good thing came out of that night," Annie said.

"What was that?"

"I've never touched beer since. I stick to wine, and rarely do I have more than one glass."

• • •

The nursery door opened, and a woman entered carrying a little girl dressed in a puffy red dress. She had a colorful holiday bow in her hair. A tall man in jeans accompanied them.

"Lindsey!" Annie said, getting up. "Look at you." She reached out to touch the toddler who was suddenly shy, and buried her face in her mother's dress.

"We were on our way to grandma's, and since we were driving right past the hospital, we decided to stop, and let you see how great our girl is doing."

"I know who you are," Phillips said. "You're one of our ECMO miracles. Wow! She looks great."

"Nobody can believe she was ever sick, and on that ECMO pump. She brought you something, Doc," her mother said.

She put the child down, and the little girl looked timidly at the doctor. Annie could see the scar on her neck. The child crept forward and reached out to Phillips. She dropped something in his hand, and jumped back to the safety of her mother's arms.

"It's a pig. We remembered about your research. One night when Lindsay was so critical—" The mother stopped speaking as her eyes filled with tears. "You kept us sane telling us about your research."

"There's something written on it," the man said.

Phillips turned the small bronze pig over, and read the inscription out loud: "*God bless the little pigs who save the little children.*" In a soft voice, he said, "Thank you."

The mother picked Lindsay up, they waved a quick goodbye, and were gone.

Jeffrey came in signaling frantically to Annie, as he pointed to the door.

"Kerry's parents are scrubbing in."

The Dawsons came into the nursery and stopped at the desk.

Addy Dawson was a slender, fragile blonde, who had been studying to be a dietician. She had dropped out of school when Kerry was born. She was wearing a frilly, red, white, and blue sundress, and a string of delicate pearls. The delicate scent of her perfume filled the air. Immediately, Doctor Phillips began to cough. He turned away and covered his mouth.

Magic had been sleeping under the desk, and came out when Phillips started to cough.

Mr. Dawson jumped back and said, "I don't think that dog should be in here."

"We've had him a long time," Phillips said. "He's an indoor dog, our watchdog, and he's very clean."

"He's still a dog."

"He thinks he's a doctor," Annie said.

Phillips took Annie by the arm, "Would you please excuse us, Mr. Dawson. The charge nurse and I haven't had a thing to eat today. What with the storms and sick babies. Why don't you go see Kerry? She's had a rough day."

Addy sagged against her husband. "Did the storms scare her?"

"No, that's not her problem. It's her lungs. She can't breathe. She's very critical. Have you been able to talk about her today?"

Mr. Dawson nodded, but said nothing as he took his wife's arm. They went toward Kerry's cubicle. Addy was already crying.

"Let's go," Phillips said. "We need a break."

Annie had no desire to go anywhere with Phillips. She had a strong feeling of impending doom whenever she looked at him.

"Hey Mackenzie," Phillips yelled. "Take charge for Annie, will you?"

He pulled Annie through the nursery doors that were still propped open. Annie took the narcotics keys from around her neck and threw them to Mac.

Annie had not seen Phillips outside the nursery in months. He had not attended any of the hospital's fund-raising events, or staff dinners, that were held in May of each year. She felt strange as she followed him to the elevators.

• • •

The lobby was full of patients and visitors. A movie was going on at one end. They both stopped to stare at the large photo of the missing child. Phillips was hugging his chest tightly as he commented, "What do you think happened to this kid? Do you think the mother was lying?"

"I don't know. I always think the worst when a child is missing. I hope there will be a happy ending to this story."

"Is there a happy ending to any story?"

"I hope so."

They went on to the cafeteria in silence. Annie got a bagel and tea. Phillips got a banana, a cheese sandwich, and coffee. The cashier looked at them with raised eyebrows when Phillips paid for both meals. Annie had forgotten her meal ticket.

Phillips pointed to an empty table in the staff-only area.

Annie sank gratefully into the padded chair. It felt wonderful just to relax and sip at the scalding tea. There were bursts of laughter from a table of interns, and Annie turned to look. They appeared excited, and their laughter was uplifting. They were just beginning a career, she was ready to end.

One group of nurses sat near the patio. The door was open, and she knew that some were sneaking out for smokes. Nothing ever really changes, she thought.

She turned to Phillips. He had not touched his fruit or sandwich. His eyes were closed, and he was rubbing his shoulders, first one, and then the other. He was wearing his old glasses, even though he had worn contacts for the past few years.

He opened his eyes, saw her looking at him, and started to speak.

The Rabbi interrupted them. "I'm so glad to find you here Doc, my laptop conked out, and I've lost some data."

Annie tuned out the computer discussion and turned her attention to Max. He was five now, a happy child with dark eyes and curly black hair. He was dressed in red shorts and a white top, personalized with his name. He wore brown sandals, just like his father, and was carrying a stuffed white rabbit.

"What's your rabbit's name?" Annie asked, as she reached out to pat it.

"Pokey," he said. "I have a real rabbit at home, but I can't bring it to the hospital."

"That's too bad, because I love rabbits. When I was a child, I had one too. Its name was Alfalfa. He hated carrots."

Max's eyes widened with surprise, and he laughed out loud. His father had his hand on Max's shoulder the whole time he talked to Phillips.

There was a page for the Rabbi, and he and the child hurried away. Max looked back at Annie, and waved his stuffed animal in the air.

As Annie waved back, a young man dressed in a light-blue suit approached them. He was carrying a sleeping infant in his arms.

"Hello," he said. "I'm Joe Barnes, the new chaplain." He nodded to Phillips, who seemed to recognize him.

"Annie Barker, NICU," she said, and realized that this might be the last time she used this introduction.

"This is my son," he said, in a proud voice. "My wife is still in line getting our food. She just arrived from California, yesterday. We're a family again." He was clean shaven, with a regular haircut. Married, Annie thought, and my nurses are going to be unhappy. They had expressed to her, that they hoped he was single.

He asked Phillips several questions about the No-Code policy.

Phillips suddenly reached out his arms to take the sleeping baby.

"He's three-weeks old today," the father said. "Not sleeping through the night though."

Phillips looked down with an expression of sadness. "My girls were once this small. They are completely dependent at this age." He carefully touched the light brown hair.

"I know," said the chaplain. "He sure lights up my world."

"He'll grow up too fast," Phillips said. "You'll turn around, and he'll be a big kid, and not needing his daddy nearly as much." The chaplain finished jotting down some things that Phillips had told him.

Phillips handed the baby back as pain flashed across his face.

"I've been counseling the Dawson family," the chaplain commented.

As the two men talked, Annie kept her thoughts on Phillips. She remembered his early years. He had a temper, but rarely used foul language. She had never seen him deliberately cause an intern pain, or shame anyone. They had often shared long grueling hours of overtime, together. He was not married then, and was in love with his job. He had picked up extra shifts, whenever possible, saving for a sports car.

There had been times when he goofed off, like everyone did. She remembered one incident: The transports had rolled into the nursery one after another. Critical babies make doctors jumpy, and they were all arguing with the nurses. An unfamiliar intern had covered, and was making all kinds of errors. Annie had beeped Phillips. There had been no response. She had then paged him STAT. She finally had to call in the night chief. When the crisis was over, she had gone looking for him. She walked into the call room without knocking. There he was—in bed with an ER nurse. Annie had seen her once, driving his new red Corvette. The nurse had covered her head with the sheet, but Phillips, with a sheepish grin, had just looked at Annie, and said nothing.

"You didn't answer your beeper," she said. "You were needed in the nursery."

His beeper was lying on the floor. He picked it up, and they could see it was off.

"Turn it on," she said, and walked out.

He appeared immediately in the nursery. They never spoke of it again.

But Jessie's death still haunted her. *Why had he ignored that dying baby?* If she was ever to have peace of mind, she had to have it out with him.

The Muzak was playing softly. It was Chopin. They watched the chaplain walk away.

The strangest look appeared on Phillips' face—a dreadful sadness.

"I always wanted to play the piano," he said, and looked at his hands.

"You're never too old to learn. Take some lessons," Annie replied.

He closed his eyes, and laid his hands on the table. "It's too late for me." His words were chilling. He opened his eyes, as he inhaled deeply. Annie feared what might be coming.

"I've got cancer." He looked small, broken, afraid.

"What?"

"Cancer . . . I've got cancer." The lines around his mouth deepened, showing his suffering. He popped more pills, washing them down with coffee.

"Pain pills," he said. "Percodan, I've had to take a lot, today." He rubbed his shoulder in a slow, circular motion.

"Cancer . . ." Annie whispered the word, just as her mother had done, when she learned it was killing Annie's father. A word you coupled with 'death sentence.'

Phillips was sick—dying. She wondered how she, a nurse, had missed it?

"It started in the prostate . . . an old man's cancer. Now it's in my bones . . . in my lungs."

The sound of laughter surrounded them. Annie wanted to stand, and shout that someone was in pain. She had the urge to run—to distance herself from this reality. Then, the nurse in her took over.

"Tell me about it."

"I found out a few months ago, during a routine physical. I thought I was just tired. I was putting in sixteen-hour days, what with my lab work. When I lost weight, I just figured I wasn't eating right. My doctor drew a lot of blood, I think he knew. I had a bone scan—the works."

He was pulling his sandwich apart. When Annie said nothing, he went on. "I needed to tell someone."

Annie reached out, and placed her hand over his. His hands were those of a sick man.

"I had a furious need to be famous," he said, ". . . and rich. It was stupid." He stared at the table. "I've done some terrible things lately . . . out of anger . . . trying to save myself. I don't want to die." He was spent.

"Have you told Molly?"

"No . . . you're the lucky one." He stared at Annie. "The last few weeks, I've been such a lousy husband . . . and father. I didn't want to burden them."

"Why are you telling me?" she said. She wanted to put her arms around him—tell him that he was not alone—make him understand that he had to tell Molly.

"Honestly, I don't know. There's something about you today, Annie, something so genuine. You always try harder than everyone else. Maybe . . . because I used to be like you. I used to care."

He played with his sandwich. "I keep thinking about what you said. You'll be leaving, and you won't even know how big a hole you'll leave in this place." He rested his head in his hands. "We used to be friends. You used to like me."

"I still like you," she said. "I just couldn't figure out why you had changed so suddenly. You have to tell Molly. She deserves to know the truth."

"I've only been able to think about myself. I've got to tell Molly, but every time I see her, or the girls, I think . . . they'll be left alone. I haven't been able to do that yet."

Annie was still stunned, and groped for the right words of comfort. She felt weak, nauseated, she wanted to vomit. She saw a nurse at the next table, looking with suspicion. Annie leaned over and kissed Phillips on the cheek. He looked up startled. "You're going to ruin my reputation."

Phillips' beeper went off. The operator called: *Code Blue in the NICU.*

"Kerry's crashing."

They jumped up, Phillips knocking over his chair. They took the stairs. "Can you do it?" he yelled. "I'm right behind you." She wondered if he could do it.

At the top of the second flight of stairs, they were breathing heavily. Phillips' face was whiter than she thought possible. At the next flight, he leaned against the wall. His face was covered with perspiration. Annie was afraid he might collapse. He went on, and she followed. They arrived at Kerry's cubicle.

Mackenzie looked up with relief. Fancy and Doctor Johnson were working frantically. Someone was calling out numbers. Annie stood with her back to the wall, her soul unprotected from this new insult. Guy was hand-bagging, trying to force air into Kerry's lungs.

Everyone looked to Phillips as he took over the code, calling out orders, between ragged breaths.

Fancy was crying as she held Kerry's head. Mac taped a gastric tube to the side of the baby's face. Someone came up to Annie and whispered, "They said you had run off with the devil." Annie motioned for silence.

Tess went and put her arm around Kerry's mother, who stood sobbing in the doorway. Annie could not look. It would be like driving a needle into her own heart. She looked at Phillips. She willed him to save this baby—one more time.

"Heart rate's down to forty," Dr Johnson yelled. "I can't get it up." There was panic in his voice. Phillips and Annie glanced at each other. Kerry remained blue.

Annie leaned harder against the wall. The room whirled, the voices mute in her ears, as the staff worked in slow motion. They fought for every second of her life, for this was the essence of their being. The monitor wailed.

"Don't let her die," Kerry's mother screamed. "I've changed my mind. I can't let her go, not yet." Her voice trailed off as she sobbed. Phillips called out orders.

The heartbeat slowed to thirty, then twenty. Johnson pushed the drugs as fast as they were passed. The intern, Kathleen, was recording. Phillips took a syringe from Mac, and plunged the needle into Kerry's chest—into her heart. The crib rolled. Fancy reached out to steady the respiratory tech.

They could hear the mother sobbing. Mr. Dawson stood outside the cubicle, tapping his fist against the wall, his head down.

When Kerry's heart rate fell below ten, Phillip's reached out, and turned off the monitor. He motioned for everyone to stop. He put his stethoscope on Kerry's chest and listened for a full minute. It was over. Kerry was dead.

Kerry's mother made her way to the bedside. She was shaking, not making a sound. She reached out and gently touched the baby. "Mommy's here, my angel, mommy's here."

Mr. Dawson stood beside his wife. He put his arm around her, and gently placed his other hand on Kerry's head—and touched his baby for the first, and last, time.

The staff left the cubicle, and Annie closed the blinds.

Annie dialed the nursing office to report the baby's death. Phillips sat in the corner filling out the death certificate.

Voices picked up in pod one. Monitors hummed. Everyone still had a job to do.

The Dawsons were left alone with their pain.

4:30 p.m. The Subbasement

Jessie's father sat on the floor, and watched Bubby play with the toys scattered around them. Some were broken, but the child did not seem to mind. He would bring a toy to the man, and want to play. Jessie's father did not know how to play.

Stark, vivid memories of his childhood came back to him. He had been sent to the orphanage the day before his sixth birthday, the day of his mother's funeral. The home was run by the Catholics. Donations always fell short of the children's needs. They received a personal toy at Christmas and got a new set of clothes on their birthday. They received a winter coat and boots, every other year.

He remembered the toy chest in the playroom, where they were sent, when it was too cold or wet to play outdoors. Any toy that was bright, interesting, or new, ended up in the hands of the older boys. There were a lot of bullies, and being small for his age, he was a victim.

People from across the country, came to adopt the girls, but the boys usually remained until they were sixteen.

Once, a man from California came to adopt a family of five girls. He brought balloons for every child.

He remembered now, watching Bubby at play, how he had loved that balloon—shiny, bright, and yellow. He had played with it until dinner time, when he tied it to his cot. After dinner, he returned to the room, just in time to see an older boy, walking up and down, breaking the balloons.

He had tried to protect his balloon, but the bully was stronger. He poked the balloon with a fork, the pieces scattering on the floor. He kept those pieces under his pillow, until a sister had found them, and taken them away.

"Milk," Bubby said, interrupting his thoughts.

"I've only got water, kid." He refilled the bottle with water.

Bubby lay on the floor and drank from the bottle. As he kicked at the floor, he said, "Mommy has Kool-Aid. I want mommy."

The man finished his last beer. "Mommy's gonna come soon. You have to wait for her right here." The child only nodded, and went back to the toys.

He noticed that the pajamas were drooping, and went over and tied them up. "Listen Jessie," he said. "I have to leave for a few minutes."

The toddler's face puckered up. "I'm Bubby. I want my mommy."

He smiled at the boy, while putting on the scrubs, and the long white coat. "Yes, Bubby, I'm going to go and find your mother."

"Doctor?" Bubby said, and he pointed to the rumpled white coat.

"Go back and play, kid."

While the boy was busy with a toy, Jessie's father took his gun from his pocket and removed the plastic that covered it. He paced the room, muttering to himself. Something was nagging at him. *It was Mary.* Mary was asking about this child. *Mary? Where are you?*

Mary's pinched features appeared. Her lips moved as she spoke. He could see the little crooked tooth he loved. He stopped and cocked his head to hear her voice. *"Take him to his mother."*

He leaned against the wall, and watched the toddler. Jessie was playing with a large, colorful ball, rolling it around on the floor. A kaleidoscope of colors exploded in his thoughts.

He was back at the orphanage. It was early evening. He had come in from outdoors, hungry for the usual supper of hot, thick soup. Two of the bigger boys caught him, and dragged him behind the kitchen. They forced him to eat a rotten potato. They shrieked with joy, as he gagged and vomited.

The next day he ran away. It was October, and the weather was chilly. The nuns did not issue the winter coats until November, and he had only his light quilted jacket. He had walked out into the countryside, and fallen asleep in an old barn. He was ten years old and alone—always alone.

He was jolted awake, when the ball hit him in the face.

"Play with me."

"I can't play right now, Jessie. I have to do something."

"I'm Bubby." The child sat down on the floor, and began to suck his thumb.

4:30 p.m. The Park

Biggs walked through the neighborhood around the park, Magic lumbering beside him. He saw the dog limp when he went over broken branches or uneven ground. He stooped and patted the great head. "You're my best friend. I'm going to miss working with you something awful."

Houses along the streets were damaged. A number of roofs had gaping holes in them. Broken windows were everywhere.

Biggs showed the toddler's picture and asked, "Have you seen this boy?"

"Ain't seen him," one man said. He had just crawled from under a damaged car, and left an oily fingerprint on the picture.

A few people answered that they recognized the picture from the news, but had not seen the child in the neighborhood. Biggs made his way back to the hospital.

In the lobby they waited for the police dog that was coming to sniff the small red tennis shoe, before the search of the neighborhood.

5:30 p.m. The Nursery

Annie sat in the nursing station and finished the paperwork on Baby Boy James. No family members had come to see the baby, and his remains had been taken to the morgue. She hated this part of the job. *And how many times must she write 'baby boy' James?*

She knew the father would not be coming. He was on a military base halfway around the world. A man who had left his family to fight for his country, would find no family waiting, when he returned.

Annie had asked Mac to take some pictures of the baby. They would make a small album of keepsakes with the baby's name card, and ID bracelet. They would file it away, for it was likely that someday, the father or a grandparent would come to ask about the brief life. Someone always came—eventually.

Jeffrey was behind in his work, and he was busy sorting lab slips, and placing them on charts.

Kerry's death had eased the nursing shortage on the unit. The glass had been replaced in pod one, and the air conditioning was now working properly. With the humidity down, it was comfortable for the staff, and nobody complained.

Phillips came and asked for some blank paper. He was walking with the shuffling steps of an old man.

Annie had suggested that he call the night chief, and ask to be relieved. "You don't have to tell him everything. Just say you are ill," she said.

Phillips took the paper from Jeffrey, went to sit by the wall, and began to write.

"Imagine," Jeffrey said, "if this whole day had just been a dream."

Phillips did not respond. He folded his paper, and put it in a brown hospital envelope. He wrote '*Molly Phillips*' on the front, and added the words, '*Please Forward.*' He put the envelope in the outgoing mail container. He sat off to the side, listless and shivering, looking strangely changed.

The chaplain came in, and sat down by Annie. "I'm sorry I didn't make it to the Dawson Code. I was in the E.R. with a trauma victim's family." The chaplain stared intently at Phillips. "Are you all right, doctor? Is there anything I can do to help?"

Phillips waved the notion away and said, "How can you believe in a God, when you see all these children in pain?" His face was shiny with perspiration under the fluorescent lighting.

The chaplain sighed. "There are days when I doubt Him. This is one of those days. Then I hold my newborn son, and it helps to keep me sane. I look for God in all the children's faces. Sometimes I find Him." What a comfort for him, Annie thought, as Jeffrey came back into the station.

Jeffrey said, "I'm taking a fifteen-minute break. There's a new unit clerk on the sixth floor who needs some help." "Is she cute?" Annie asked. Jeffrey blushed, and hurried away.

The chaplain laid his hand on Annie's shoulder. "Take care," he said, and quickly left the unit.

Phillips asked, "How about you Annie, do you believe in God?"

She waved away her melancholy. "I believe in good. I believe that this is all there is. I just never made much fuss about God. Jackson doesn't either. He's interested in Buddhism."

"Well, do you think there are bad people?"

"I think there are people who do bad things. I don't think anyone gets up in the morning and says, 'I'm going to be bad today.'"

Fancy came into the nurses station. She had cried so long over Kerry, that all her makeup was gone. She had the fresh-scrubbed look of a new student nurse.

"I don't feel too good."

"Why don't you go home?" Annie asked.

"Did the nursing office say I could?"

"No, I said you could."

"And I'll second that," Phillips replied.

"I haven't told my husband yet about the ruined car."

"Why don't you take a cab home, and charge it to the hospital. That's what I intend to do," Annie said.

"But you live fifty miles away."

"So? I won't state my destination when I pick up the voucher from security."

As Fancy left through the automatic doors, Magic entered. Clearing the doors, he loped into the nurses station and sprawled at Annie's feet. She reached out to pet him. She would miss this dog.

"Sorry old fellow, I'm out of treats. My pockets are empty. Even the ice cream is gone."

Phillips was on the phone. He talked for a few minutes and hung up. "Libby's in the delivery room." He then pulled his gold pen from his pocket and handed it to Annie. "Because this is your last day, I wanted to give you something. You should go out in a blaze of glory. Don't let the hospital give you one of those stupid teas. They are for old people. You're not old, Annie. What a gap you're going to leave in this place."

Annie was overcome with emotion. She knew he was trying to make amends for his behavior over the past weeks. "You write with this pen all the time," she said.

Guy came running in and handed Phillips a blood gas sheet. He studied it, looked at Guy's happy face, and gave him a thumbs-up sign. Guy took the sheet and left as quickly as he had come.

"Annie, this is going to be my last day too," Phillips said. He sagged on the stool, as if just speaking, was exhausting for him. "I won't need that pen where I am going. You know, I can't take it with me."

Recollections of their conversation in the cafeteria came back. She wanted to say something reassuring, but then Guy was back pulling Phillips to his feet. "We need you back in the ECMO pod."

Annie did not go with them. She watched the stooped frame of Phillips being led away by Guy whose healthy erect body dwarfed the doctor.

She sat motionless and looked at the elegant gold pen with Phillips name engraved on it. It felt heavy in her hand. She slipped it into her pocket.

Jack Biggs came into the nursery carrying an armload of pizza boxes. "It's a gift from Channel Five News. They sent them over because they knew we'd had a terrible day. The administrator gave the okay—we can have it on the units."

Phillips returned, along with Jeffrey, who declared, "We can't eat in here."

"Sure we can," Annie said. "I imagine that everyone has forgotten the ice cream by now. They can fire me if they want to."

Phillips nodded and remarked, "You're too old to fire, Annie." He had the proud look of accomplishment on his face. "The ECMO kid is doing great. I talked to his mommy. She's going to be discharged later today, and she'll be here after that."

"Have some pizza," Biggs said.

"I'm not hungry," Phillips said. He went to his usual stool.

"How old are you, Annie?" Jeffrey said.

"None of your business," she replied, and she playfully poked him in the chest.

"Don't abuse the staff," Jeffrey ordered, and then raised his arms in mock defense.

"Any news on the missing boy?" Annie said.

"Nothing yet. We're getting ready to search the hospital again," Biggs answered.

They had an impromptu celebration. The nurses took turns covering each other, so they could all enjoy the pizza. Even the lab technician, who had been gathering blood samples, took off her gloves, washed her hands, and joined them. Magic cleaned up any bits that dropped on the floor.

Biggs was on the phone talking with the police department. He watched the activities, smiling at the staff. When his beeper went off, he turned to the dog. "Come on Magic, we've got more work today, old buddy. You'll get your much needed rest eventually." He patted the dog.

Annie went to check on Deltiffinase. She had no visitors today except staff members. Someone had hung a new dress on her stand. Annie figured that it must have been Mac. She made a quick round of the nursery and returned to the station. Phillips was talking on the phone, and she noted the serious look on his face. He searched on the desk and found a pen and began writing. He had always ranted and raved when he couldn't find his gold pen. She felt uneasy. *Why did he give it to me?*

Phillips hung up the phone and turned to her—with a look she understood.

"It's a transport," she groaned.

Mackenzie and Tess came into the station.

"Damn," Annie said. "We're getting a transport, and I just sent Fancy home."

"You girls aren't going to believe me," Phillips said.

"It's a transport, right?"

"Three," he said.

"Three!" Mackenzie screamed.

"They're dumping on us big time from the university. Sending over a set of triplets—already two-weeks old. They need cardiac workups. They don't want to wait, since two have already developed murmurs, and they think the other one will, too."

"Why today?" Annie asked. "Can't they wait until tomorrow when we have a full staff?"

Phillips sighed. "They can't wait. I said they could come, and they are on their way. University needs space for some new admissions, too. They have six women in active labor." Suddenly, his face took on a chalky color, making his shabby beard stand out. He was breathing heavily as he staggered out of the unit, almost falling.

Annie saw the horror on Mackenzie's face. Mac started to go to him, but Annie grabbed her arm. "No," she said, softly. "Leave him alone. He'll be all right."

After Phillips went through the double doors, Annie took Mac aside. "He's having some medical issues today." She hated to withhold the truth from Mackenzie, but she had promised Phillips.

"I've got to find Jeffrey," Annie sighed. "He's going to have a load of paperwork."

6:00 p.m. The Hospital Lobby

Jack Biggs paced in front of the main lobby elevators. He pulled a comb from his pocket, and sliced it through his hair. The guards were regrouping for another search of the hospital—the second since the child had gone missing. Magic was lying close to the reception desk, resting.

Biggs rubbed his stiff neck as he paced and thought about taking an early retirement. He could retire without a problem; he already had twenty years of service. After today's events, it did not seem like such a bad idea. The hospital wanted him to train a new dog. They had even offered a large bonus. If he accepted their offer, he would have to farm Magic out to someone else. The old dog was not one to share the lime light.

"We're all here, Sir."

Biggs counted twelve guards, ten regular, and two called in for overtime. They had each walked past Magic, and given him a soft pat on the head. The dog rested, but his eyes were alert as he watched Biggs.

The guards stood at relaxed attention as Biggs looked them over. Most had children, and they lamented the missing child. Three were women. The diminutive blonde, on one end, was a favorite of Biggs. She was tiny but tough. He had trained her himself.

"I'd like you to listen to Sergeant Thomas from the city police," Biggs announced. The sergeant was well-known to most of the older guards. Both of his sons had been born with Cystic Fibrosis, and had been hospitalized frequently. Thomas, a short brisk man with a pockmarked face, spoke in a congenial manner.

"Are you positive that you've searched every nook and cranny of this place?" He stood with his hands on his hips, his cap tilted at a precarious angle. "It's hard for me to believe that nobody saw this kid leave the lobby." There was murmuring, and exchanged glances.

"Is there any chance that a staff member might have taken him?"

"Not a chance," Biggs said.

"It's always a possibility," the sergeant said. "We have to think of every conceivable scenario, and follow through." Everyone nodded.

"You've searched every room thoroughly?" Sergeant Thomas scanned the guards' faces.

A new guard, still on probation, shifted nervously. He had not thoroughly searched all the storage rooms in the subbasement. Too much partying, the previous night, had given him stomach cramps and diarrhea. Part way through his search, he had stopped to find a bathroom, and had gotten behind. He nodded in agreement with the rest of the guards.

The sergeant turned back to Biggs. "Take over."

Biggs began to assign areas to be searched. He paused, and said, "We've been on our feet all day. I think you could use a break. Take thirty minutes, and get something to eat and drink."

The information desk was swamped with calls, parents continuing to check on their children. One irate father brought an overnight bag to the hospital. He

said, "I'm not leaving until they find that missing kid."
He made the six o'clock news.

The staff was feeling the stress. Too many visitors
interfered with normal hospital duties. Two television
trucks were parked on the hospital's front lawn. They
were broadcasting live from the lobby. When a nurse
or doctor came within range, a microphone was stuck
in their face.

"Excuse me, doctor. Could you give a statement?"

"Pardon me, nurse. Do you think the child is still
alive?"

The ICU lounge, on the second-floor, fared no better, crowded with weary parents and visitors. Magazines
were scattered, wastebaskets overflowed, and someone
had placed a half-eaten hot dog in a potted plant. Two
mothers contested the use of a free phone: a pigtailed
brunette suddenly pummeling an obese redhead—the
redhead having the size advantage, the brunette having a nail file. A few cheers attracted security, and they
were separated. Jack Biggs arrived and dismantled the
phone.

• • •

In the subbasement, Bubby played, and waited for
the man to bring his mommy.

In the emergency room, Bubby's mother sat in a
small rocker, mute, holding her swollen jaw. She refused food and drink, and ignored the reporters.
Scarcely beyond childhood herself, she grieved alone.

6:40 p.m. The Nursery

The staff was busy, preparing for the arrival of the triplets. There was a standing admissions joke: "We're getting triplets!" This time it was not a joke. There was grumbling—change of shift arrivals were always looked upon with trepidation.

Annie was in the nursing station with Phillips, who sat at the desk. He seemed indifferent to the unit activity. Annie saw him pop more pills, and worried that he might pass out.

Jeffrey arrived with three new charts. He said, "I couldn't believe it was happening. The elevator just kept going to the subbasement. Apparently someone removed an out of order sign."

Annie glanced at the clock. There was no way she would get off on time. Jackson would be worried. She called home, and got the answering machine. He was not home yet. She left a message.

Doctor Johnson stood in the hallway, trying to explain an x-ray report to juvenile parents. They were smiling, and pretending to understand.

"Everything's ready for the trio," Mackenzie said, coming into the station. She boosted her bulky frame onto a high stool, and propped her feet on the rungs. Her eyes were still red from crying about her dog.

Annie smiled and pointed to her ruffled anklets. *Mac was unique.*

"I'm going to take a few days off," Mac said, brushing the hair from her face. "I called home. Mother said the doctor had given Nixon a sedative, and he was sleeping at her side." Her face revealed a sad acceptance of the inevitable.

Annie just nodded.

"And some people think it's easier to have pets than children ..." Mac's voice trailed off as she rested her arms across her chest.

"Well, you can't sedate a child and let it lie at your feet," Jeffery said, "but I agree, pets are special. Someone has to hold my cat's head when I give him medicine, or he bites me."

"Some of those people in the lobby should be locked in a loony bin," Annie said. She wanted to steer the conversation away from Mac's dog.

The phone rang and Jeffrey answered: "Transport is five minutes out." Although it was against policy, they propped open the automatic doors.

· · ·

They rolled in—one after the other—as each nurse took up her new charge. Three warming beds waited in the first pod.

"Didn't take long to fill this pod again," Guy said. He had relocated the former patients when the window was replaced.

Annie admitted the smallest, and sickest, of the three, the only boy. His tiny chest moved irregularly. The tinge of blue around his lips indicated a cardiac problem. Phillips followed Annie, along with Doctor Johnson.

Annie said, "Breath sounds are down on the left. Want me to call x-ray? The tube may have shifted."

"Damn it, that's my job—I'm the doctor," Johnson said, but he was grinning at Annie, as he took over.

Annie was pleased to see his increased self-confidence. Earlier, he had seemed terrified. Now, battered and bruised by the storm—and by Phillips—he stood in front of her, acting like a pro.

Phillips listened to the baby's chest. Annie noticed his drawn face, the eyes, sunken in their swollen sockets. Still, his thin white hands were calm. He looked at Johnson. "Annie's right, as usual. Let's just go ahead and re-tube. This kid is ready to crash. We can get an x-ray later. I don't want any more deaths today." He spoke in a monotone.

Johnson smiled at Annie. He looked professional, even with his black-and-blue forehead. Guy helped with the respirator.

The x-ray confirmed a perfect placement of the endotracheal tube. Doctor Johnson attempted to praise Phillips, but the older doctor simply waved him away, and went back to the nursing station.

One of the transport nurses waited, while Annie finished a task. "I've got a present for you," she said, and held out a Polaroid picture. Annie saw a smiling Libby, with a naked infant in her arms.

"She's doing great," the nurse said. "They suctioned the baby really well, before they let him take a breath. He hasn't had any problems. No signs of aspiration."

Annie thanked her, and took the picture to Phillips. He gazed at it for a moment without commenting, and handed it back. He was bringing the triplet charts up to date.

Annie informed the staff about Libby. *One of their own . . . delivered . . . the baby healthy . . . the mother okay.* For Annie the day was finishing up better than she had hoped. She checked on Deltiffinase, who was simply growing and developing as she should—one day at a time, the way preemies were supposed to do.

Tess came looking for Phillips. She had a smile on her face, and Annie knew the news was good. "The ECMO kid is doing fantastic." She waved the blood gas sheet in their faces. "At this rate, he'll be off the machine before midnight."

Phillips looked up, and appeared momentarily uncertain. He coughed, before looking at the sheet. He studied it, then without looking up, told her to have Johnson make the change.

"Maybe you'll be home before midnight," Tess teased. When he still did not acknowledge her, Tess stopped smiling.

Annie followed Tess out of the station, gave her a quick hug, and whispered, "He's exceptionally tired today, and his allergies are bothering him. You'll have to forgive him."

Annie wanted to scream over the intercom: "The man is dying! Can't you see it?" Instead, she kept his secret, just as he was keeping hers.

Guy came in, and motioned Annie to the hallway. He was beaming, and could barely control his excitement. He grabbed her hands. "You aren't going to believe this."

"Well, tell me."

"Terry took Billy and picketed in front of the house of the homeowner. He put a sign on Billy that said: 'I want to live here.'"

"He did that?" Annie had never met Terry, but had spoken to him on the phone.

"Some of the neighbors came, and asked what was going on. Terry told them the story. One went and talked to the owner, and threatened to call the news."

"And?" Annie couldn't help smiling.

"The owner came and talked to Terry, and to Billy. He said we could have the house—at the original price."

"Great! Maybe you have a guardian angel, after all."

"There's something else, I never told you, Annie." He grinned, and said, "I never told you that Terry was white."

"Well, you are full of surprises, today."

Annie hugged him. She knew he would be good for the child.

Guy danced away, and ran back up the hallway. She envied him, taking on the world like he did. It was so much easier to do nothing—to never rock the boat.

She used to have strong medical convictions, but there were so many changes now—dramatic changes. *Some changes occur too quickly.* She wanted things to slow down, to stay the same. *But things change.*

"Hey, Annie," Mackenzie yelled from pod one. "Can you help me draw up syringes for the night shift? I threw the others out, when they expired." Annie joined Mac.

With her back to Phillips, who was checking out the triplets, Mac said, "What's with him, all of a sudden acting so chummy with you? Am I missing something?"

"Yes," Annie whispered back. "He asked me to have an affair, but I refused." Mac burst out laughing, and Annie had to laugh, too. She found new energy when she was around Mac. They both drew on sterile gloves, and began to draw up syringes.

Annie's mind was flooded with the events of the day: the baby deaths, the storm, her encounter with Mark Blair, the missing child, and Phillips. Her thoughts kept coming back to Phillips—but there was nothing she could do for him.

"I've always wanted to ask you something," Mac said. "Now don't get angry at me." Annie was immediately on guard.

"I saw you with Doctor Blair, earlier," she said. "Weren't you guys a twosome, a long time ago? I was on another unit at the time, and the nurses would gossip, especially after his wife left him."

"Nothing ever got past you, Dear Mac. Would you believe that I almost went to Texas with him?"

"Really? Didn't we hear that he left suddenly, and then his wife died?"

Annie sighed. "He didn't leave suddenly. He was supposed to leave. He had finished his residency. Her death had nothing to do with his leaving. Tell you what, let's do lunch sometime, and I'll fill you in on all my sordid past."

"I would love to have lunch with you. We could talk about something besides nursing. I like Blair—always did. I'd never do anything to embarrass him—or you."

"Then, it's a date."

"Why didn't you marry him?" Mac couldn't resist one last question.

"I was quite young then—and wild. It took me years to grow up. I had decided not to marry, ever. Then, Jackson came along."

"How did you meet Jackson?"

"I was moonlighting in the emergency room at the medical center, trying to pick up some extra money. It was right before Thanksgiving. Jackson was delivering a load of frozen turkeys, and dropped one on his foot. It broke his toes."

Mac laughed. "Not too romantic, but very unusual."

"I had to call his dispatcher. The guy laughed, hysterically, when I explained what happened."

"What a riot."

"Jackson found out my name, and called me every day, for a week. Then, when he came though the city, he would call," Annie paused. "We really had nothing in common, except we both liked cats. I had two, and he had three. I married him to give my cats a father . . . I've had no regrets," Annie smiled.

Phillips was pacing at the window behind them. Tess brought a blood gas sheet, and handed it to him. This time, he made some banter, but Tess was serious.

Phillips went to the wall, and turned on the x-ray illuminator. He began to study the x-rays on the triplets. They were all waiting for the cardiologist, who was still in the operating room.

Phillips stood bathed in the eerie light. It shone on his white hair, giving it a yellow cast. He had taken off the red sweater, he had been wearing, and now had on a scrub top, that was too large. Annie watched him carefully. By this time tomorrow, his resignation would be official. *Would anyone be told about his illness?* Annie turned to Mac.

• • •

Through the opened double doors, a man entered. He was dressed in scrubs, and a long white coat. He hurried past Jeffrey, and two nurses, to the first pod.

Annie recognized him—*Jessie's father!*

She started to take a step forward.

Phillips turned from the x-rays. He frowned, as if trying to recognize the man.

"Yes?" Phillips reached out his hand.

A violent shiver ran down Annie's spine.

Jessie's father was five feet from Phillips. He said something. Annie couldn't make it out.

Mac turned from the drug cabinets. Her mouth opened, but no words came out.

The man took his hand from his pocket.

Annie gasped, her knees starting to buckle.

Phillips, his hand still extended, his eyes wide open, started to smile—

"You smile at me, you baby killer?" the man said.

Jeffery stood behind the man. Annie saw his open, frozen mouth.

Jessie's father laughed once—his hand shook a little.

Annie screamed, "Magic," and instantly realized he was not there.

She grabbed Guy's cart. With a desperate lunge, she pushed the cart towards the man, crashing it against a sink, near Mac.

The shots rang out—

The first shot—hitting a monitor—the screen exploding.

A second—tearing into Phillips—the impact propelling him into the wall.

A third—striking Phillips in the face above the eye. He crumpled to the floor.

The man grunted, and turned to Annie, his gun pointing straight at her.

As Annie took a deep breath, he shook his head, moaned, and dropped the gun. It bounced, and thudded against Annie's shoe.

With arms flailing, he turned, and ran through the open nursery doors.

Annie kicked the gun away, and ran to Phillips.

He lay on his side, his right arm outstretched, the hand open, his eyes closed.

"Jeffrey!" she screamed. "Call a code, get the trauma team, get security, oh God, oh God, oh God . . ."

She pulled linen from a stand, and held it over his chest wound.

Doctor Johnson came running, disbelief on his face. He fell to his knees, and searched for a pulse in the neck.

"He's still breathing," Mackenzie said, standing over Annie.

"I feel a pulse," Johnson said—his voice shrill. "Get me some scissors!"

A young surgeon came running into the pod. Two more doctors arrived, one of them was Blair. Annie got the emergency drug box, and tore off the seal. She felt like her heart was bursting, she couldn't breathe. One of the doctors snatched the box from her hands.

The trauma team arrived, and she stepped back against the wall.

"Everyone back but the trauma team," Blair thundered. His eyes met Annie's. She saw the terrible truth, but refused to accept it. She backed out of the pod. She had to get away.

She could hear the team behind her, but she could not look in their direction.

People were standing in the hall, parents and staff. She quietly asked them to return to their babies.

Annie went to help Mackenzie move one of the triplets. The bilirubin light had protected the baby from the exploding monitor glass.

"Jeffrey, get bio-med to look at that monitor." She was afraid of a fire.

I am still in charge of this madness, she thought. She swallowed back a sob, turned, and looked towards Phillips.

He was already intubated, and a doctor was hand-bagging. Blair had inserted a chest tube, and the doctors discussed their options. She saw Blair insert a needle into an artery in the neck. A city squad arrived with a gurney. They placed Phillips on the cart, for transport to the University Hospital. As they wheeled him out, Annie saw his left hand start to jerk.

"Oh, Mac," she said. "He's starting to seize."

His pain . . . his revelation . . . Oh, God, he doesn't deserve to die like this.

She turned to Mac, and they held each other and cried.

Jack Biggs came running into the nursery. "I ran all the way from the cafeteria. Someone thought they saw a man carrying a small child." He paused, gasping for breath before he could go on. "Did anyone see the shooter? Which way did he run? Did anyone recognize him?"

"Yes, yes" Annie said. "He's the father of a baby who died here."

"Why would he shoot Phillips? Did he say anything?" Biggs was still in disbelief.

"He said something about a baby killer," Annie said. Annie remembered Jessie's death, but was not going to bring it up, not now.

"Maybe he blamed Doctor Phillips," Mac said. "There were some rumors that Phillips had come too late to the baby's code."

Annie was surprised at Mac's remark. She thought that no one else had noticed Phillips being late.

"That baby was tragic," Mac said. "He died a nasty death."

"Phillips did run the code," Annie said. Or should have run it, she thought. The father must have blamed him. She had blamed him.

"The man looked spooky, like a robot," Mac said.

"There's the gun." Annie pointed. It was still lying against the wall, where Annie had kicked it. She wanted them to stop talking about Phillips. He could not defend himself, now.

"The police will want to talk with each of you," Biggs said. They went into the nursing station.

Jeffrey sat mute at the desk. He was still in shock. When the telephone rang, he did not reach for it. Mac answered.

Annie went back to pod one, and got some cotton balls. She soaked them with peroxide, and stooped to wipe the blood off her shoe. She spotted an object lying on the floor, by the wall. It was the little bronze pig. Phillips must have dropped it when he fell. She put the pig in her pocket. It was her last link to Phillips. It clinked against the gold pen.

Annie walked to the desk and dialed the nursing office. Her legs were unsteady, and there was still the ache in her heart.

. . .

The guards fanned out to search the hospital.

"Look in every room, every closet. Open every door, locked or not." Biggs picked the petite blonde, and a tall black man, a former high school football star. "Come with me. We'll start in the subbasement."

"It's spooky down here," the blonde said, as they stepped off the elevator. They heard the noise from the kitchen. There was laughter and soft singing. Those in the subbasement were isolated in their own little world.

The first door Biggs unlocked was a storage area for pharmacy. Shelves of bagged solutions and canned formula lined the walls. There was no place for a person to hide, and they shut the door and locked it. The second room was filled with beds and mattresses. Some folding chairs were stacked in wheeled carts, and there was nothing behind them. There was no sign of the man, or any evidence that he might have been there.

The third room was unlocked when Biggs tried the knob. "What the hell?" he said, as he swung the door open. The scene caused his pulse to race. There were toys scattered over the floor. A pair of men's pants, spattered with paint, had been flung down carelessly. Empty beer cans, and a baby bottle, lay in the corner.

One isolette, against the wall, had a door open on the bottom. Biggs checked inside. He found a piece of lamb's wool—soaking wet—and a small red tennis shoe.

"He's been in here," Biggs said. He raised a stricken face to the other guards. "The kid has been in this room, and someone has been here with him. My God, he must still have the boy." He thought about what to do next. "I'm going to get Magic." Three minutes later, he was back with the dog.

"I wonder," Biggs said. "I remember early this morning, when some empty isolettes were still in the lobby. If the child climbed into one, that could have been how he got out of the lobby, without being seen. They always bring the dirty ones here. They never clean them on a holiday."

He paced and thought. "We've got to find the guy. We have a guard at every exit. I don't think he can get past them, especially with the kid. Someone would recognize him." Biggs got on the phone, and talked to the captain of the city police.

"Where could he hide that we haven't looked?" Biggs thought out loud.

"And where nobody would see the child?" the blonde added.

"He may still be in this basement somewhere," Biggs murmured.

They headed toward the furnace area. They walked past the noisy air-conditioning compressors, unable to converse due to the roar of the machinery.

"Wait," Biggs said and paused. "I forgot about the outside courtyard. We haven't used it in years, but I know that sometimes the smokers sneak out there while on duty." The two followed behind Biggs, until they came to a door. He reached out and tried the handle. The door was unlocked.

"They do this sometimes, fix it so they can get back in without a key card. He may be out there."

He took a deep breath, and motioned for everyone to be quiet. He told the blonde to hold tight to Magic's collar, and not to let go unless he gave the word. He eased the door open.

They saw a man sitting on a stone bench, holding a small child. The man stared back at them. The boy clung tightly to the man's arm, as the guards entered the courtyard.

The man stared at Biggs with eyes that were strangely calm. Biggs looked into the blue eyes of the child. It was Bubby.

Biggs motioned for the others to stay back, as he went forward. He saw that the child clung to the man, like he knew him. The scene burned into Biggs brain. As long as he lived, he would retain it.

Biggs turned and watched for Magic's reaction. Magic simply whined for a second, and then sat, in a tranquil fashion. Biggs knew the boy was not in danger. Magic was too calm.

"You must be Bubby," Biggs said, very softly. He didn't want to spook the boy or the man.

Bubby looked surprised. "You have my mommy?"

"Yes," Biggs said. "Mommy wants me to bring you to her." He reached out to loosen the man's grip on the child. The man held tightly, and appeared confused.

"Bubby's mom is waiting for him. Please let him go."

The child turned to the man holding him, and patted his face. "Mommy wants me." The man started as the child again touched his face. He then let out a painful cry, as he held on to the child more fiercely. "Jessie," he said. "My Jessie!"

"Did you find Mary?" the man asked, in a begging voice.

"Yes," Biggs said, not knowing who Mary was. "We found Mary, and these nice people are going to take you to her." The man nodded, and slowly released the boy. He then suddenly fell to the ground, and drew himself up in a fetal position, calling out for Mary.

"Bubby," Biggs said, as he lifted the small, dirty toddler into his arms, "I'm so glad to see you." He felt all over the small form. The child appeared to be uninjured. "How did you get away from your mommy?"

"Don't know." Bubby nodded his head with a serious look. "Mommy lost me."

"Take over," Biggs said to the blonde, and he handed her his gun. "I'll send a stretcher."

They all looked at the man curled on the ground. He was shaking all over.

"Alcohol withdrawal," the blonde whispered to Biggs.

Biggs carried the child from the courtyard into the hospital. The little arms clung tightly to his neck. He went down the long hallway, and up the stairs, to the waiting arms of a mother.

8:20 p.m. The Nursery

Annie signed off the narcotics sheet, while Mackenzie gave the nursing report. The night nurses were buzzing with questions. They would go unanswered for now, at least until the hospital official report came around, specifying what information could, and could not, be released.

"There's a Valium missing," Joan said.

Annie sighed. "I'm not surprised that something's missing. Fancy probably used it on Kerry. You'll have to give her a call at home. I think her chart is still on the unit, so you can go over it with her."

After the shooting, Mac had jumped in, and taken over most of Annie's duties. It amazed Annie, that Mac was so efficient. Mac had always claimed that charge duty made her too flustered.

Annie rubbed the back of her hand across her mouth. Her lips were chapped and dry. Her voice was hoarse from talking to the police detective. She had to go over and over, the scene with the gun.

Joan sighed, and said, "I can't believe everything that has happened in this place today. I've only worked here for six months. Nobody told me that a hospital could be such a dangerous place to work. I thought about calling off, but I couldn't think of a good excuse."

Annie locked the narcotics cabinet and gave Joan the keys.

"Isn't it wonderful that they found the missing child and he's okay?" Joan went on.

The little voice had boomed over the loudspeaker: "*This is Bubby. I have my mommy.*"

Annie stood at the desk, as Mac finished up the report. The day was playing over in her mind. She felt numb, and vulnerable.

Jeffrey was signing out to the night unit clerk, when the telephone rang. He listened to the brief message, his childish face clouding over, as he hung up. They all waited.

His lips quivered and he could barely speak. "Doctor Phillips died a few minutes ago." He started to cry and Annie went to him. He said, "I've never seen anyone shot before. Why did it happen? You can't just walk into a hospital and shoot a doctor."

"We are never completely safe, Jeffrey." She wanted to weep at the injustice.

Mac said, "We'll never know for sure why he did it, unless the police can get the man to talk. They say he is catatonic now. I think it was because Jessie died."

Annie glanced around the room. It would never be a place of refuge for her again. She had seen the injuries, but had hoped the outcome would be different.

"Oh, why did it happen?" Mac said.

Jeffrey began to put the paperwork in order.

Annie wished that Phillips could have known about Bubby.

She turned to leave the nursing station, and saw the brown envelope in the outgoing mail with Phillips' handwriting: *Molly Phillips.* Suddenly, she had an idea. She picked up the envelope, and headed for the nurses lounge. It was unoccupied, but she continued into the bathroom. She turned on the light, and locked the door.

She sat on the commode and pulled the gold pen from her pocket. She would put it in the envelope for Molly. She undid the metal clasp on the envelope. She removed the letter, and unable to help herself, read what he had written.

Dear Molly,
I need to say goodbye. I've been a very selfish man. All the good things in my life are connected to you and our girls. Please remember that. You crowd my thoughts today. Forgive me for not taking your phone calls. My head is pounding in pain, and fatigue rules me. I've done terrible things lately out of sheer fury, and I do regret them.
Molly, know this one thing, this is not your fault. This is my decision.
I love you and the girls.
P.

Annie knew it was a suicide note. He was going to kill himself. Oh, God, she saw all the signs now. He had been so distant, and he had given away his gold pen. And all those drugs he was taking, he was not thinking clearly. He was not in his right mind.

Tears poured down her cheeks. She thought about his last few hours. He had been so alone, and he had shared with her, but she had been of no help to him.

She hugged the letter to her chest and tried to decide what she should do. *Should she put it back in the envelope?* It would be terrible for Molly to get this letter now—Phillips was already dead. It would serve no purpose. This would only hurt Molly and the girls. Annie tore the letter into bits and flushed them away. She was not sure it was the right thing to do.

The staff would talk about Phillips' last few weeks, the way he had changed, his hateful manner, his heavy-handed way with the interns. They would not remember the same man she had known for so many years. This was one last thing she could do for him.

She slid the gold pen into the envelope and closed it. The pen would go to Molly and the girls. She would keep the little bronze pig.

She remained in the bathroom for several minutes. Someone approached and knocked on the door. "Busy," she called out. She then blew her nose, and smoothed her hair. She looked in the mirror. The face of her mother stared back at her.

It had been almost ten years since her mother had died. She remembered her mother's last words: "*I've had a hard life, Annie, but I've always managed to go forward, and I have no regrets. You can go forward, or you can look back and suffer, but you can't do both.*" She smiled at her mother's image. "You were a wise old bird," Annie said.

Annie went back to the nursery, and replaced the brown envelope in the outgoing mail.

She saw Guy approaching. "What a day," he said, "I'm going home." He hugged her. "See you tomorrow, old friend." He smiled and was gone.

Mac had her black bag slung over her shoulder, and a large bag of dirty linen in her hand. She plopped the linen down, and grabbed Annie for a hug. "Don't forget to call me about lunch," she said.

"Awful lot of hugging going on," Jeffrey said. His face was still sad.

"We couldn't have done it without you." Annie hugged him, and so did Mac.

Annie decided to walk the nursery hallway, one last time. She passed Kerry's darkened cubicle. There was not a sign that a baby had ever struggled for life in that room. She thought about Kerry's mother, and wondered if she would sleep at all tonight—or ever sleep again.

She stopped at Alex's door. Alma had volunteered for a double shift. Her back was to Annie. She was giving Alex a bath, and clean linen was piled on the stool. She had water all over the crib and the floor. She was singing to Alex, in a tinny voice. He was smiling and waving his arms.

Annie walked to Deltiffinase's bedside. The baby was lying quietly awake, a small ebony thumb in her mouth. Annie blew her a kiss.

She went back to the ECMO pod. The baby was off the pump, and they were letting him wake up. He was moving his arms and legs. His mother was there, pale-faced and proud, sitting beside him in a wheelchair.

The staff had gathered by the bedside of Jill, one of the twins from the failed home-birth. They were ready to see if she would come off the respirator. Doctor Grayson, the night chief was talking. He had quietly taken over Phillips' duty. He looked up, saw Annie, and nodded. He towered over everyone. Annie had spent a thousand hours at his side. It was good to see him, one more time, standing there, and teaching the new interns.

The baby squirmed on the warming bed. Her eyes opened for a moment, but the lights were dazzling, and they closed.

"And now, Baby Jill," Grayson said, "it is time to pull the tube, and see if you can breathe all by yourself." And so the tube was pulled, and she was ready. Jill tried a breath or two. It didn't seem to tire her. She tried another and another. Soon she began to breathe in a regular rhythm. Her heart rate speeded up. Still it was steady. The cool mist once again blowing into her face.She was warm. Her body was pink. She found her fingers, and began to suck loudly. She drifted in and out, away from all the noise, the happy voices. Her father's laughter brought her fully awake.

Everyone cheered.

• • •

Annie was alone, by the time she got to the time clocks. She inserted her card for the last time, and replaced it in its slot. She came to the darkened office of the nurse manager. She slipped a sealed envelope under the door and smiled.

She went slowly through the main lobby. A baby dressed in a faded yellow short-set was crying. The baby was fat and healthy. The elderly woman holding it, looked at Annie, and Annie smiled.

Annie walked out into the late evening. It was muggy, and the setting sun was still a brilliant orange. She had to shade her eyes to find her cab.

She saw a little boy playing in the sandbox, in the park. He was pouring a can of soda pop into the sand. His mother smoked a cigarette, and paid no attention.

Annie handed her voucher to the taxi driver.

"That's a long way," he said. "And the hospital is going to pay for it? Wow."

She fastened her seat belt, and watched as a child released a silver balloon into the air, from the back of his wagon. She heard the child's excited shrieks, as the mother tried unsuccessfully to stop the balloon's ascent. It rose like a free spirit, drifting away, high above the damaged trees.

The taxi raced down the street. Just before the freeway, the driver swung towards the old state route.

"Take the freeway," Annie yelled.

"Can't," he yelled back. "Didn't you know? There was a bad accident on the freeway. A car went over the median, and into the path of a semi. The truck turned over. I saw the Life-Flight lift off with the driver, as I was coming to your hospital."

Annie stopped breathing, and tried to ignore the screaming in her head. Finally, she got it out: "Did you see the truck?"

"Yeah, and I heard on the radio that the driver died."

"What color was it?" She inhaled raggedly and waited for his answer.

"The truck?" He took the unlit cigar from his mouth and frowned. She watched his face in the mirror as he tried to remember. She saw the recollection come with his wide grin. "It was black and silver."

She could breathe again, and she fell limply back against the seat.

Jackson would be home and waiting.

Waiting for her.

His truck parked in the driveway.

His truck was red.

Acknowledgements

My profound thanks go to my husband, Frederick. My gratitude, to my friends in the nursing profession, and to the doctors who continue to care for these tiny babies. A special thanks to my children, Heather, Shane, Brett, and Brittney, and to my grandchildren, Megan, Mickey, Liam, Ethan, Kacey, Elliot, and Julian. And I am grateful for the memories of all the babies I was privileged to hold in my hands.